JOHN WILSON

Based on the screenplay by

XIAOMING YAO

ORCA BOOK PUBLISHERS

First published in North America in English
by Orca Book Publishers in 2018 as *The Third Act*.

The Third Act
第三幕

The Third Act originally published in Chinese Language
by Sichuan Fine Arts Publishing House Co., Ltd.

Library and Archives Canada Cataloguing in Publication

Wilson, John (John Alexander), 1951–, author
The third act / John Wilson; based on the screenplay by Xiaoming Yao.

Based on the screenplay The 3rd act.
Issued in print and electronic formats.
ISBN 978-1-4598-1967-2 (softcover).—ISBN 978-1-4598-1969-6 (PDF).—
ISBN 978-1-4598-1968-9 (EPUB)

I. Title.
PS8595.I5834T55 2018 jc813'.54 C2017-907965-4
C2017-907966-2

First published in the United States, 2018
Library of Congress Control Number: 2018933715

Summary: This novel for teens moves between the
Nanjing Massacre of 1937 and the present day.

Orca Book Publishers is dedicated to preserving the environment and has printed this book on Forest Stewardship Council® certified paper.

Orca Book Publishers gratefully acknowledges the support for its publishing programs provided by the following agencies: the Government of Canada through the Canada Book Fund and the Canada Council for the Arts, and the Province of British Columbia through the BC Arts Council and the Book Publishing Tax Credit.

Cover design by Teresa Bubela
Cover images by Qi Yang/Getty Images and ViewStock/Getty Images
Author photo by Katherine Gordon

ORCA BOOK PUBLISHERS
orcabook.com

Printed and bound in Canada.

21 20 19 18 • 4 3 2 1

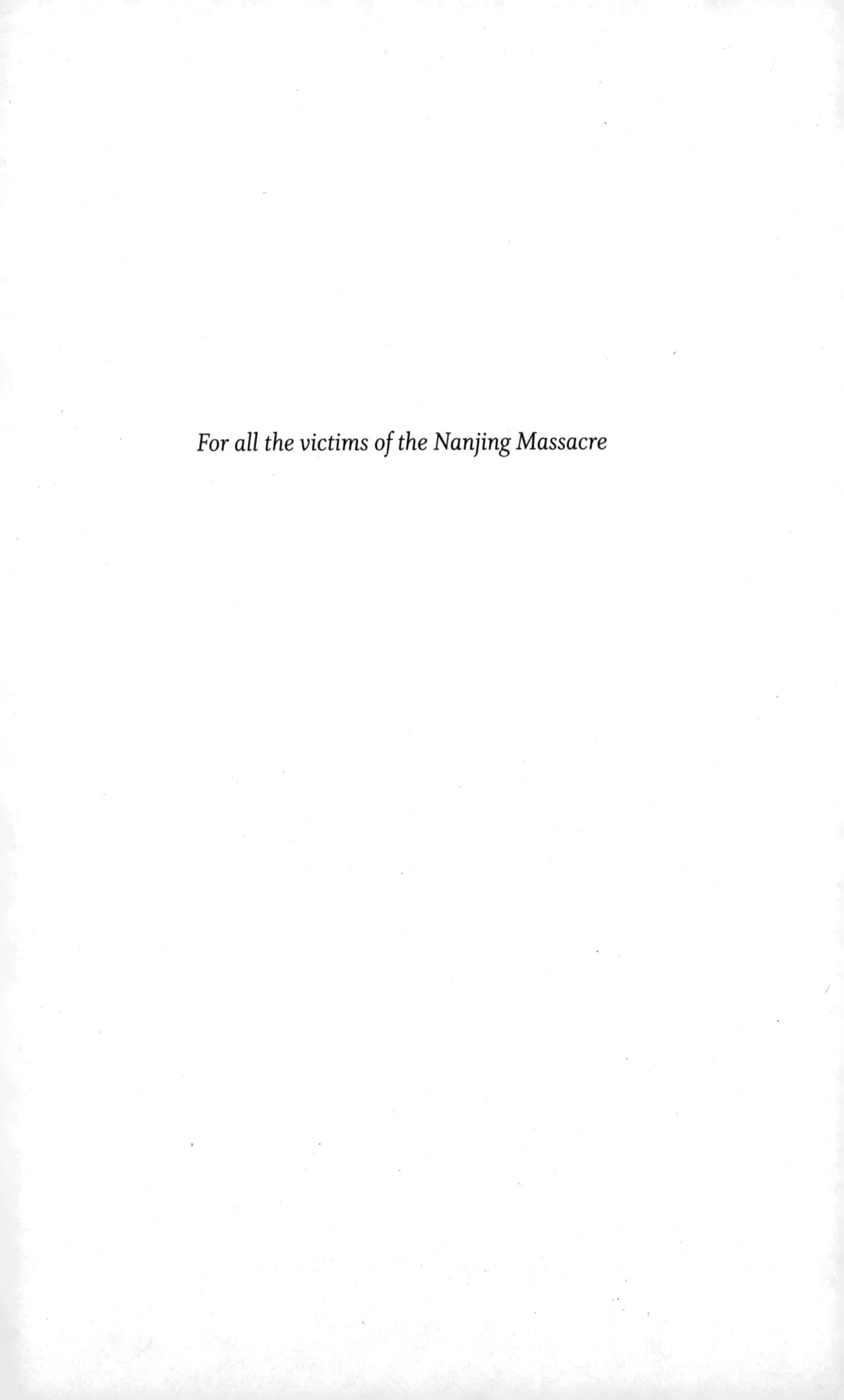

For all the victims of the Nanjing Massacre

CHAPTER ONE

Nanjing, Jiangsu Province, Republic of China
Evening, December 13, 1937

Hill Chao ducks around the corner into the shadow of the narrow alley. Flattened against the wall, he watches the squad of Japanese soldiers march past. He's in the Safety Zone, but close to the edge, and ever since the Japanese stormed over the city wall earlier in the day, no one is certain they will respect it. Hill is dressed in civilian clothes, but he's of military age, and he knows from the stories his father has told him that this puts him in serious danger.

As soon as the soldiers disappear, Hill darts out into the deserted road. He moves slowly, working his way over and around the piles of rubble and trying to avoid the bodies. He knows there must be people in the undamaged houses on either side, but they are huddled deep inside with the blinds drawn.

Hill has worked his way to the middle of the road to avoid a burning building when a bomb explodes in the next street over. The sound distracts him and muffles the noise of the plane banking along the street behind him. The first he knows of it is when the bullets chip the rubble at his feet. Hill dives to one side as the plane roars above him at rooftop height. He gets a glimpse of the red suns on the wings in the glow from the fire, and then the darkening sky is empty.

His heart thumping, Hill drags himself to his feet and continues cautiously on his way. Despite the danger, he is preoccupied. The past hours have turned his life on its head, and he has some important decisions to make.

"Thank God the worst is over."

Neil Peterson stands by the windows at the back of the balcony of the Jinling University theater, staring out over the gaping shells of ruined buildings and Nanjing's ancient city walls at the fires roaring across the slopes of Purple Mountain. The smoke from the burning city veils the setting winter sun and adds a sense of foreboding to the view. He shivers and pulls his jacket tight around him.

Lily Chan turns from the flames to stare at Peterson. Because she's almost a foot shorter than the American, she has to look up. Despite how long they've known each other, his profile, with its aquiline nose and prominent chin, still seems strange to her. He's good-looking, but his features are too big, making his long face appear cluttered. Sometimes she gazes into the mirror at her own delicate, perfectly proportioned features and wonders, If we ever had children, what would they look like?

Peterson glances down at her. "What are you smiling at?"

"I was just thinking that you look like Leslie Howard in *The Scarlet Pimpernel*."

Peterson laughs shortly. "Me? A British movie star playing a hero rescuing aristocrats from the guillotine in the French Revolution? I don't think that's my role."

Lily's smile fades. "We're all destined to play roles here—and you, a playwright, should understand best of all that no one knows what his role will be until the cast list is posted."

"It was posted this morning when the Japs came over the city wall. We're to play the part of the defeated. The Battle of Nanjing's finished."

"Maybe." Lily looks back at the mountain. "Why did you decide to stay here?"

"Why did *you*?" Peterson counters. "Anyone with enough money has fled the city."

"I have a responsibility to the drama program. I spent years overseas studying Shakespeare so that I could properly introduce his work in China. Should I give all that up now just because of this stupid war? Besides, this is my country. You're a stranger here, visiting so that you can study Guan Hanqing's thirteenth-century plays. You could have left with all the western diplomats, businessmen and journalists."

"On the *Panay*? You may not have noticed, but she's at the bottom of the Yangtze today."

"Okay, but your American ambassador and his staff left for Wuhan three weeks ago. You've had plenty of opportunity to leave. Why didn't you?"

"In case you've forgotten," Peterson says flippantly, "we're staging Hanqing's *Lord Guan Goes to the Feast* in a couple of days."

"You can't be serious about doing the play with all that's going on!"

"Why not? Most of the preparation's done. The actors are all ready to go, and the dress rehearsal's tomorrow afternoon. I admit that a few of the extras have fled, but we'll round up more. It's not as if they have to act. All they need to do is stand around pretending to be soldiers."

"I'm not sure that dressing Chinese as soldiers is such a good idea these days."

"They'll be dressed as thirteenth-century soldiers. I doubt even the Japanese will be upset at that. Anyway, Shimada's on board with the whole idea, so he'll clear it with the Japanese military."

"I don't trust him."

"Why? He can be annoying, but he's always been helpful, and his contacts with the Japanese have been useful—and will be more so now that they have won the battle."

"I know, I know." Lily struggles to put her feelings into words. "I'm just uncomfortable around him. I'll be talking to some students and suddenly feel uneasy. I'll turn around and find Shimada standing in the shadows, staring at me."

Peterson laughs. "I stare at you. You're beautiful and well worth staring at."

Lily smiles uncertainly. "It's something in the way he stares." She shrugs. "Maybe I'm imagining it," she adds, although she doesn't believe she is.

"I'll check him out. He's coming to the dress rehearsal tomorrow."

"You invited him?"

"Yeah. I want to keep on his good side and find out if there's anything in the play that will offend the Japanese who might come to the performance. If there's a problem with the soldiers, he'll tell us."

"You've invited Japanese to the play?"

"Only a few from the embassy. Shimada thinks it's a good idea, and I do too. Especially now that we have to keep on their good side. One day we may need visas out of here."

Lily doesn't look convinced, but she says, "I suppose it will take people's mind off things."

"Of course it will. It'll be fun."

Lily frowns. How can he talk about fun in the middle of a war? Doesn't he understand how serious the situation is? But she says, "Okay. We'll go ahead with your play, although I doubt we'll have much of an audience. But that can't be the only reason you're still here—and don't say it's also because of me."

"But it *is* because of you," Peterson says. Lily flashes him an angry look, and he smiles apologetically. "Okay." He looks back at the mountain, rubbing his chin. "I guess I want to write about something important."

"So you risk your life in the middle of all this"—she waves an arm to encompass the destruction around them—"to find a story?"

"That's about the size of it. You keep telling me that Americans don't understand China, that we sit in our comfortable isolation without any idea of the complex struggles faced by other nations and peoples." He turns back to Lily, his face serious. "We all live in dangerous times, even the Americans who don't realize it yet. Fascism, communism, war here, civil war in Spain—I don't want to go back and sit in my cozy office while the world goes to hell around me. I want to experience everything."

Peterson's grim expression softens into a smile. "Besides, *civis Romanus sum*. Or perhaps I should say *Americanus*—I am an American citizen. As you said yourself, the Japs don't want another incident. They're not going to harm an American playwright, even one who's not very well known. I'm safe, and if you stick close to me, you'll be safe too. Don't worry. Everything will work out fine. There'll be a couple of days of mopping up after the battle, and then we'll all settle in under our new masters. When it's all over, you can come with me to the States. I'll be a famous playwright, and you'll be a famous actress, maybe even in the movies."

"Don't be so certain the world will turn out as you want," Lily says as lightning flashes among the rolling clouds above the hill. The accompanying thunder is indistinguishable from the deep rumble of the artillery. "There's an old prophecy that says when Purple Mountain burns, Nanjing will be destroyed."

"And it's come true," Peterson agrees. "We've been bombed every day for the past three months. Most of Nanjing's a ruin. But at least that's going to stop. The Japs won't want to bomb their own troops now that they're inside the city."

As if to contradict him, several artillery shells explode across the city suburbs to the south.

"I don't think that's what the prophecy means. A city's not just roads and buildings—they can be rebuilt. It's the people who make this a living place." Lily is interrupted by a sudden burst of heavy machine-gun fire from the riverbank. "But what if all the people die or are driven away? Who will rebuild Nanjing then?"

"Damn, you're depressing. Look, the Japs are harsh—no one's denying that. There's already been too much destruction and death, and the occupation's not going to be a bundle of fun. But the fighting will end. Even now the Chinese soldiers are either fleeing or tearing off their uniforms and finding civilian clothes to wear. Like I said, there'll be a few days of chaos and then the Japs will set up an administration while their army heads upriver for the next battle. All we have to do is hang tough."

"And what about the hundreds of thousands of refugees crammed into the Safety Zone with us?" Lily leans her forehead against the window glass and peers down at the ramshackle tents and shelters crowded into the open ground in front of the bell tower. People shuffle around nervously, looking up whenever gunshots sound nearby. Here and there, small cooking fires flicker in the deep shadows.

"The Japs don't care about them. They're poor and they're harmless—mostly old men, women and children. It'll be tough to feed everyone for a while, but that Nazi businessman John Rabe and the men on his committee seem to have that under control. In a few days everyone will go home and we can get on with our lives."

"You Americans!" Lily's voice sharpens with anger. "Everything's easy for you. You say we all live in dangerous times, but you don't understand what that means. It's theoretical to you. You want to experience the world, but the only world you truly know is a safe, organized, rational place. You imagine the rest of the world as a slightly messy version of that, with just enough danger to make it interesting.

"But China's not like America. We live on the edge. We have spent thousands of years peering into the abyss of war, famine and pestilence, praying that some petty warlord doesn't ride over the hill and slaughter our children, or that an unimaginable natural disaster doesn't destroy all that we've worked for. We don't have the security you have in Boston or San Francisco."

Peterson turns to Lily and places his hands on her shoulders "Natural disasters happen everywhere. Remember the San Francisco earthquake?"

"Oh, yes!" Lily says scornfully, shrugging his hands off. "A *major* disaster! And how many people died—a few hundred?"

"Around three thousand," Peterson answers.

"The Shaanxi earthquake in the sixteenth century killed eight hundred thousand." Peterson tries to interject, but Lily holds up her hand. "If that's too far in the past for you, is six years ago recent enough? That's the year the Yangtze—the river a few hundred yards from where we're standing right now—and the Yellow Rivers flooded." She takes a deep breath. "Four million people died in the floods and in the famine and disease outbreaks that followed. So don't argue natural disasters in my country."

"Okay, okay." Peterson holds up his hands in mock surrender. "But I'm really not talking about that. I'm talking about the practicalities of here and now." He puts his arm around her shoulder and pulls her in close. Her head nestles under his chin. "The Japanese aren't savages, Lily. They've had a sophisticated culture for the same thousands of years that you've been teetering on the edge. In fact, if you go back far enough, their culture derived from China."

"Okay, Neil, but what's your point?"

"My point is that two civilized nations can go to war, sure. But we've moved on from Attila the Hun and Genghis Khan. Literature, music, theater—these things are universal. They cut across national borders. Look at Shimada. For all your misgivings about him, he's going out of his way—even in the middle of this war—to try to get Hill a permit to study traditional theater in Kyoto. We're safe here. I promise you. In a few weeks we'll look back on today as the end of a bad dream."

"I truly hope so," Lily says, "but—"

"There you are. I've been looking all over."

Lily and Peterson draw apart and turn to see Hill coming up the balcony stairs. He's wearing loose pants and a padded jacket against the cold. His face is pale and drawn.

"Where have you been?" Lily asks, stepping away from the window.

"I've been talking with my father. He arrived two days ago from Shanghai and made it into the Safety Zone only yesterday." Hill rubs a hand across his forehead and blinks. He looks close to collapse. He glances nervously at the fires on Purple Mountain.

"Let's sit," Lily suggests, taking his arm and leading him to the nearby seats. Peterson moves to the side and lights some candles in holders along the wall. There has been no electricity for three days now, and the generator hasn't been switched on yet for the evening. Either that or it has run out of fuel. The candles flicker but do little to dispel the gathering gloom.

Lily and Hill sit down side by side, Lily still holding his arm. Peterson stands behind them in the half-light and stares thoughtfully toward the empty stage.

"You should get some rest," Lily says.

"I will, but not yet." Hill shakes his head. "There's something I need to do."

"Is your father okay?"

Hill smiles weakly. "He's completely worn out. I found him some rice, and he's sleeping now. His journey here was a nightmare. He's not even sure how long he was walking, struggling to keep one step ahead of the Japanese. He stopped at Suzhou, but the Japanese attacked there. The same thing happened at Jiangyin, Changzhou and Danyang. He could never rest for long, and the food he carried with him was gone in the first few days. He's not a young man anymore. It was torture."

Hill lowers his gaze and blinks hard.

Sensing that he wants to talk more, Lily gently squeezes his arm and waits, but Peterson says, "He's safe now, Hill. Everything will be better in a few days."

"I don't think so," Hill says with a catch in his voice. "I don't think things will ever be right again."

"Hell, you're as depressing as Lily. It's war, goddamn it. But your father made it through. We're safe here, and things will—" Something in Hill's expression stops him in midsentence.

"My father saw things." Hill speaks so softly that Peterson finds himself leaning forward to catch what he's saying. "Deserted villages. Buildings burned out, and blackened bodies scattered everywhere. Ditches filled with the stripped and mutilated bodies of girls and women, their bellies ripped open and their throats cut after the soldiers had had their pleasure with them. Rows of decapitated bodies, their heads arranged neatly on their chests. Not a single thing alive. A landscape as silent as at the beginning of the world—or at the end."

Hill drops his gaze and for a long moment stares at the floor. Eventually he shakes his head and continues. "Outside Changzhou, Father joined a group of several hundred refugees—women and children, old men and wounded soldiers. All of them, like him, fleeing from the Japanese. They traveled together for several days, sharing what little they had.

Whenever a Japanese plane flew over, they took shelter in the ditches beside the road, but no one attacked them."

Hill stops again, and Lily and Peterson wait. When he speaks his face is grim in the candlelight. "Then a Japanese patrol came out of the woods on one side of the road. The officer in charge was polite. He said they were looking for Chinese soldiers. An old man stepped forward and respectfully said there were mostly families in the group. Any soldiers were unarmed and wounded, and no threat to the Japanese. The officer nodded and smiled, then pulled out his pistol and shot the old man in the chest."

Hill shrugs off Lily's arm and stands up. "Everyone was lined up along the roadside," he goes on, his voice gaining strength as he speaks. "The soldiers picked out every male between ten and fifty years of age, regardless of whether they were wearing a uniform or not. Mothers were on their knees, pleading for their sons' lives, but it did no good. All the men and boys were herded down to a nearby farmer's pond and machine-gunned. Those who survived were bayoneted. The bodies were thrown into the pond."

Peterson stares at Hill, his eyes wide. "Ten-year-olds?" he stammers. "Your father must be mistaken."

"There's no mistake," Hill replies, his expression cold and hard. "How much longer can you go on believing in the secure bubble of American safety? How much longer can you believe we're not surrounded by savagery? That there are not roadsides where ten-year-old boys are bayoneted and their bodies thrown in a stagnant pond? Your comfortable little

American world is surrounded by chaos and horror, so don't tell me we're safe here." He turns on his heel and strides out of the theater.

For several minutes Lily and Peterson stand in the flickering candlelight, staring at the empty doorway. Lily is crying silently.

Finally Peterson says, "I can't believe it."

"You don't *want* to believe it. What do you need—photographs?"

Peterson recoils at the violence in her tone, but Lily's anger vanishes at the sight of the shock on his face.

"I'm sorry," she says, stepping forward and embracing him. "I didn't mean to hurt you. What kind of nightmare are we living in?"

"We're safe here," Peterson repeats, patting her comfortingly on the back.

She pulls away from him and wipes the tears from her cheeks. "What did Hill mean?"

Peterson looks at her questioningly. "I don't understand."

Lily chews her lip before answering. "He said there was something he needed to do, but he never told us what it was." She moves toward the door.

"Where are you going?"

"I want to make sure he's all right." She pauses in the doorway and looks back at Peterson. "A moment ago you thanked God that the worst was over. But you and your God are wrong. The worst is just beginning."

CHAPTER TWO

Ashford, Ohio

Present Day

Pike Xhou's head jerked up as the tires on his red Subaru WRX whined over the rumble strip in the center of the road.

"Shit!" He shook his head to clear it. "Gotta stay awake."

He eased back into his own lane and reached over to the passenger seat. His hand rummaged through the empty chip packets and torn candy wrappers like a small, frightened animal looking for shelter.

"Shit," Pike said again.

He lifted a Cheetos bag and tipped the crumbs into his mouth. Most of them landed on his cheeks, rolled down his grubby sweatshirt and came to rest on his ample belly. He made a halfhearted attempt to brush them off before sweeping the garbage from the seat into the debris on the floor from his previous snack attack. He drained the last dregs of his grape-flavored water and tossed the bottle.

As soon as he hit a gas station, he'd pick up a couple of energy drinks. That should see him to where he was going. The last thing he wanted was to end up in a ditch. This car was worth money. Not that it was his money—his father had given it to him as a birthday present three months ago—but Pike had put a lot of effort into the aftermarket accessories: the RalliTEK turbocharger, dark-tinted windows, eighteen-inch titanium rally wheels, stealth exhaust and high rear spoiler. He'd waited weeks for the work to be done. That was why he was taking the roundabout route home this morning—he just wanted to enjoy it.

Even worse than trashing the car would be word of it getting back to his parents in China. Eastern University was a small school in a small town. It was tough to get away with anything, and he was living on the edge as it was. He was barely passing and narrowly avoiding getting kicked out. His parents didn't know the half of it, although his father had suspicions. He'd warned Pike a couple of times not to let his grades drop and to keep out of trouble. And while Pike didn't give a damn about a good degree or a worthwhile career, he certainly didn't want the money spigot to be turned off. Wrapping his expensive new car around a tree after an all-nighter would certainly do that.

Then there were the contents of the backpack lying on the seat behind him. Pike glanced at the speedometer and let up on the accelerator. The needle on the gauge dropped back by ten miles an hour, to just over seventy. A speeding ticket wouldn't be a good idea either.

Pike eased the car smoothly around a tight bend as the sun hauled itself above the eastern hills. He smiled to himself. Even with a hangover, this was a beautiful machine to drive. One day he'd do a road trip out west—to Nevada or somewhere with open roads and little traffic—and have some fun. Maybe that's what he would do this summer. What was the point of living if you didn't have fun?

Pike was still smiling at the thought of going flat out on some desert road when he looked in the rearview mirror and saw the police cruiser. He instantly slowed down, even though he knew he was doing the speed limit. How long had the cop been there? Had he clocked him when he was going a little faster? Had he seen Pike weave into the other lane? Pike hadn't had a drink for hours, so he was pretty sure he was under the limit. *Oh, shit! The backpack.*

Keeping the car going as straight as he could with one hand on the wheel, Pike reached into the back. It was awkward—there wasn't much room between the seats. He felt around. Where was the damn backpack? He kept his head as upright and still as he could. There it was—a strap, at least. He pulled, and the pack slid onto the floor behind his seat. Taking a deep breath, he reached down and shoved it as far under his seat as he could. He swallowed hard and flicked his eyes to the rearview mirror—the cop was still there, about a hundred yards back. Did he see Pike's head bobbing around? Pike glanced at the speedometer. His speed had dropped while he was fighting with the backpack, so he accelerated, pulling slowly away from the cruiser. He was okay. He would be all right.

Then the red and blue lights flashed, and the long wail of the siren rose and fell.

Pike felt the burn of bile in the back of his throat as his stomach tried to eject all the junk he'd ingested over the last twelve hours. He forced himself to swallow it back. His mouth was dry. Sweat ran down his sides, and he was suddenly aware that he hadn't showered for a long time. He pulled the car over onto the hard shoulder.

In the side-view mirror he watched the cruiser pull in behind him. The cop killed the siren but kept the lights flashing. He sat in his car for what seemed like an eternity—checking the Subaru's license plate, Pike supposed. Well, there should be no problem there. He hadn't even had the car long enough to get a parking ticket yet.

Pike had to force himself not to turn and try to push the backpack farther under his seat. His palms were slippery with sweat. He wiped them on his pants and then returned them to the steering wheel, gripping it so hard that his knuckles turned white. He was breathing fast and shallow, and his stomach was lurching. Why had he done it? Why, why, why?

At last the cop appeared satisfied. He stepped out of his cruiser, closed the door, adjusted his hat and the gun on his hip, and walked slowly forward. He stood slightly back of the window, knocked on the glass and said, "Please roll down your window, sir."

Pike pressed the button and gave the cop what he prayed was a sincere, friendly smile.

"This your car?"

"Yes, Officer. I just got it a couple of months ago, and it's been in the shop since then. I haven't had much chance to drive it. I hope I wasn't speeding." He knew he was talking too much, but he couldn't help it. "I'm just heading home from visiting some friends and thought I'd take the long way home. It's such a beautiful morning."

The cop didn't look like he wanted to talk about the weather. "License and registration," he demanded.

"Sure." Pike lunged toward the glove compartment.

"Slowly," the cop warned, his hand resting on his gun.

Swallowing hard, Pike pulled out the registration papers. He handed them out the window and slid his driver's license out of his wallet.

The cop took his time checking everything. Pike was convinced he'd smelled the sweat and stale alcohol on him.

"Where's home?" the cop finally asked.

"Ashford," Pike replied. "I'm a student at the university—physics."

The cop nodded. "The car must be worth a few bucks."

"Yeah," Pike agreed. "My dad bought it as a gift for getting good grades." The good-grades bit was a lie, but the cop wouldn't know that. Pike had learned that telling people he was doing well at university impressed them.

The cop peered into the backseat. Pike held his breath.

"Your backpack's fallen on the floor," the cop said.

"Yeah." It was all Pike could trust himself to say.

"I saw you," the cop said.

Pike swallowed and gasped a lungful of air.

"You were leaning back, trying to get the backpack out from under the seat."

"Yeah," Pike agreed.

"That's why I pulled you over. It's a real dangerous thing to do. You wouldn't believe the horrors I've seen because someone bent down to pick up his cell phone or pull something out from underneath a seat. The main cause of accidents is driver distraction. You want something in your backpack, pull over and get it. You'll live longer that way."

"I will, Officer. Thank you."

The cop handed Pike's papers back through the window. Pike fumbled them into the glove compartment and closed it.

The cop didn't move. "Now would be a good time," he said.

"What?"

"To get whatever it was you wanted from your backpack. Now would be a good time."

"Sure, sure." Pike unbuckled his seat belt and opened the door. He hoped his knees would hold him.

The cop stepped back. "Be more careful."

"I will, Officer. Thank you again."

The cop walked back to his cruiser, climbed in and killed the lights.

Convinced his heart was about to give out, Pike opened the back door and hauled out the backpack. As he closed the door, the cop pulled onto the blacktop. He waved as he passed.

Pike leaned heavily against the car. He was shaking and felt like bursting into tears. Nestled at the bottom of the backpack, and feeling like they weighed a thousand pounds, were a Ruger SP101 revolver and a box of ammunition.

"Good morning." Tone leaned over and kissed Theresa on the cheek. A shaft of dawn sun highlighted the riot of black hair spread over the pillow. "The sun's up. Time to get moving." The only response he received was a grunt as she pulled the blanket over her head.

For Tone, sunlight through the bedroom curtains was a cue to get up, get organized and get on with the day. For Theresa, it was a signal to steal another ten minutes in bed.

"You do realize we're totally incompatible," he said, patting the lump where Theresa's shoulder would be. This time he wasn't even rewarded with a grunt.

He slid out of bed, switched off the alarm on his cell phone and padded to the bathroom. He stared at the face in the mirror, scanning the well-defined chin, full lips, narrow nose and sharp cheekbones that Theresa teased could slice salami. He narrowed his dark eyes into what he considered a mysterious, sultry look. He'd always thought he could have been a movie star if he hadn't dedicated his life to science.

Tone absent-mindedly adjusted the bottles and jars of moisturizer, mouthwash, hair gel, shampoo and conditioner into ordered, evenly spaced lines on either side of the sink as he planned his wardrobe for the day. It was going to be warm, so the summer suit, a standard white shirt and the red-and-black-striped tie for a bit of color. He'd have to shine his shoes though; he'd forgotten to do that the night before.

He grabbed the robe from the back of the door and stood staring at the unmoving lump under the blankets. They had been going out together for several months, but in the last three Theresa had spent more and more time here with him. She still had a room in residence on the university campus, but she had started to hang some of her clothes in Tone's closet and use part of the space in the chest of drawers in the corner. Having to rearrange his belongings did annoy him, but it was a small price to pay for being with the most beautiful girl in the university. The last three months had been the best of his life. Tone smiled. "I'll put the coffee on," he said, as if it wasn't something he did every morning.

As the coffee machine began to gurgle, Tone threw open the drapes to let sunlight flood the two-bedroom bungalow. He peered out the window at the small yard. The untidiness of the unmown grass and the weed-filled flower bed offended him, but he wasn't about to do anything to change it. He was an organized person, but gardening held no attraction for him. What was the point of grubbing around in the dirt to make a garden neat when it would be untidy again within days? When he was rich and had his own place, he would hire people to keep things orderly.

Tone turned and let his eyes wander over the living room. He had an office in the physics department of the university, only a fifteen-minute walk away. Here at home he needed only his neat little desk beside the fireplace on which to balance his well-ordered collection of books, papers and his laptop. His PhD work on cryogenics was complete and defended, a remarkable achievement for someone of his age. All he needed to do now was make some minor editorial changes and prepare a few peripheral papers. His groundbreaking paper in the *Journal of Low Temperature Physics* had been extraordinarily well received. If he got a decent doctoral fellowship at a high-reputation school, he was on track for a stellar academic career.

Theresa spent most of her time in the university theater, but Tone had designated a work area here for her too, in hopes that she would eventually move in for good. It had a beanbag chair, a bookcase and a low table overflowing with annotated scripts and pages of scrawled notes. Tone couldn't understand how Theresa was able to work amid such clutter, but at least she was more organized than Pike.

Pike's corner of the room was a large desk completely covered with books, papers, ring binders, disposable cups and half-eaten sandwiches that were gradually turning into their own unique ecosystems. Occasionally Pike could be persuaded to remove the worst of his moldy food, but as far as Tone could see, the books and notes were rarely touched.

Tone wondered how Pike managed to scrape together enough passing grades to enable a return each semester. Tone helped him as much as he could—letting Pike look at old papers he'd written to give him ideas for his own—but there were still practical classes and in-class assignments that Pike had to do on his own.

Tone's gaze drifted to his roommate's bedroom door. It was half open. A pair of sweatpants was trying to crawl out into the corridor. So Pike hadn't returned last night. Another party that was just too good to miss.

The coffee was ready, and Tone poured two cups. One he took to Theresa and set on the bedside table. The other he sipped as he sat down at his desk and flipped open his laptop. His desktop image popped up—a cartoon of two melting snowmen, one saying, *I'm seriously thinking of getting into cryogenics*—and his email pinged. Fifteen messages, the usual dross from a night of inactivity: warnings about suspicious activity on a bank account he didn't have, ads for Viagra, notifications of another big lottery win.

Tone's rapid scan halted at the third email from the bottom. It was from MIT, the Massachusetts Institute of Technology, one of the top universities in the world—right up there with Oxford, Cambridge, Harvard and Stanford—and where Tone dreamed of doing his research. His finger hesitated on the touchpad. Was this it? What he'd been waiting for? The slightest movement of his finger would open the email and signal the direction of the rest of his life. An acceptance and he was on the first rung of the ladder to international recognition, the beginning of his life. A rejection and he would be just another PhD graduate teaching at some mediocre school and struggling with insufficient funds to carry out the significant work he was destined to do.

Tone had worked hard to get to this point. He knew he had the talent, but success was more than mere skill, and

Tone didn't believe in luck. He had planned every move carefully, selecting courses that looked good on his résumé and were taught by the biggest names in the field. He'd nurtured professional relationships that could advance him. He'd calculated every step. Acceptance would be the culmination of everything he'd done so far.

Tone took a deep breath and clicked on the email.

Dear Mr. Zhang:

It is with great pleasure that I am writing to offer you the prestigious Kelvin Fellowship in Low-Temperature Research for a four-year term beginning in September of this year.

The awards committee was most impressed by your academic record—so many accomplishments at such a young age!—and by the quality of your published research. We here at MIT take pride in…

Tone leaned back in his chair, closed his eyes and exhaled, enjoying the happiness. What an idiot he'd been to doubt, even for a second, that this was his destiny. He felt strong, powerful, in control. Everything was going as planned. He opened his eyes. How would he celebrate with Theresa? Perhaps an expensive meal out? There was that good Italian restaurant on the main drag. He'd make a reservation. They could all go to the Blue Bar early for a couple of drinks, and then he could surprise Theresa with the dinner reservation. Pike wouldn't mind being left in the bar—it was his second home anyway.

Tone's cell phone vibrated on the desk beside the computer. He glanced at the screen. Professor Seeger. He scanned the email heading. Yes, Seeger had been cc'd.

"Good morning, Kenneth," Tone said cheerfully.

"Tone, have you checked your email this morning?"

"Yes," he replied, savoring the moment.

"It's fantastic. Congratulations. Quite a feather in your cap—and in the department's, if you don't mind my saying so. To have a postgraduate from our school awarded the Kelvin Fellowship..." Seeger let the possibilities hang in the air.

Tone allowed the silence to hang. He was having fun controlling Seeger.

"Anyway," Seeger went on, "we're opening up the department meeting at ten this morning—moving it to the main hall. The president's going to be there, along with the dean and all the top brass. The media's invited. You'll be the star of the show—maybe make a short speech thanking the university, saying what a wonderful place it is to study at and how you couldn't have come as far as you have without us. That sort of thing. Okay?"

"Sure," Tone said, struggling to keep the laughter out of his voice. "I'll be there, and I'll say nice things."

"Excellent. See you then."

Tone put the phone aside.

"Who was that at this ungodly hour?"

Theresa was standing in the doorway. Even without makeup, she was beautiful. Her long black hair gleamed in the low sunlight as it fell over the shoulders of her white robe.

Tone's first thought was to go back to bed, but he pushed the idea away. "It was Seeger."

"What did he want?"

Theresa yawned, a lazy, catlike gesture that Tone found strangely arousing. Perhaps going back to bed wasn't such a bad idea.

"Do you remember when you came to America and you said you weren't sure you'd like it out east?" Tone asked.

"I remember. Too cold."

"You wanted to go to California and the sunshine."

"Yeah. That was my wish, my dream. So?" Theresa tilted her head and looked at him quizzically.

"I've got news to celebrate. Do you want to go to the Blue Bar tonight?" Tone spun his chair and began reading from the screen. "*It is with great pleasure that I am writing to offer you the prestigious Kelvin Fellowship in Low-Temperature Research for a four-year term beginning in—*"

He didn't get any farther before Theresa's arms were wrapped around his neck. "You got Caltech!" she gushed. "Pasadena's not on the coast, but it *is* California. This is great news."

Tone untangled her arms from him. "I told you I wasn't applying for Caltech. It's too small—not enough resources for the work I want to do. This is much better than Caltech."

"Where then?" She read the email over Tone's shoulder. "MIT? You're going to MIT! That's Boston! They get even more snow than we do!" Theresa stepped away from him, her eyes narrow and angry. "Is this some kind of sick joke?"

Tone forced himself to remain calm. He loved the drama in Theresa, the way she could go from bored to ecstatic in a split second, leaving his head spinning. It was tougher when she spun the other way.

"You didn't finish reading the email," he said slowly. "They go on to say that the fellowship involves spending at least six months of every year at the Kirkland Research Institute in Palo Alto. I know your geography's a little shaky, so let me explain that Palo Alto is just south of San Francisco. Yeah, it's *northern* California, and it's only half of each year, but it's the best I could do."

He couldn't avoid the sarcasm slipping into his voice, but Theresa didn't seem to notice. She was busy cycling back up the emotional scale. "San Francisco's awesome for theater. There are great acting coaches I can work with. I can get an agent. I'll go to auditions every week. LA would be better, of course, but I suppose if I'm going to hang around with you, I'll have to accept second best."

"Ha-ha. Look, I've got to get showered and dressed." Already he had decided on a dark suit and more restrained tie. "Seeger's going to make a big deal of this at the ten o'clock meeting this morning. It's going to be in the main hall. I want you and Pike—wherever the hell he is—to be there."

Theresa's expression darkened. "It'd be nice if you asked instead of ordered. Anyway, it doesn't matter. I can't be there at ten."

Tone frowned. "Why not?" It came out more harshly than he intended.

"Allen's called a meeting for ten. He's going to announce the cast for his new play. I think I've got a lead. He specifically asked for me to be there."

"Shit, Theresa, this is important to me. All the top people—and the press—will be there. It's what I've been working for my whole life, and I want you and Pike sitting beside me in the front row."

"Look, Pike can go with you this morning, and I can join you later to celebrate," Theresa said, trying to ease the tension. "You deserve this and more." She placed her arm across his hunched shoulder. "But my work is as important to me as your work is to you."

"But what you do isn't real life," Tone protested. "It's playacting. And Allen Quigley will give you the role whether you're at his meeting or not."

Theresa dropped her arm from Tone's shoulder and stood up. "Playacting! Don't belittle what I am and what I do! For me, drama *is* life! It's language, beauty, art, music, love." Anger surged through her. "And you'll get the MIT position whether you go to *your* meeting or not."

She turned and strode toward the bedroom to get dressed.

"Please come with me," Tone said to her retreating back, disgusted at the neediness that had crept into his voice.

She ignored him and slammed the door behind her.

"Shit! Shit! Shit!" he exclaimed under his breath. The most momentous day of his life, and it had started with a fight! This was the biggest thing that had ever happened to him, and she was going to miss it for some play. Why couldn't she understand how important this was?

And where the hell was Pike?

Theresa threw on her clothes with furious intensity. Tone was such a control freak! She *was* proud of his achievements, but they came at a price. True, successful scientists had to be logical, but did Tone have to apply such extreme rationality to everyday life?

Spending so much time here with him and Pike, she had become even more aware of that rationality. Tone tried to control the world around him, as if it were one of his experiments in the lab. Pike seemed to relish living at the center of a swirling cyclone of chaos. They were polar opposites. Yet there was a strong bond between them. Pike worshipped Tone, and in return Tone helped Pike with his assignments so he could survive another year. It was a thankless task, but Tone seemed dedicated to helping the one person who annoyed him the most. Perhaps control and chaos could exist only in a symbiotic dance.

Still, hanging out here with Tone and Pike was more fun than her single room in residence, and, if she was honest with herself, it felt a bit like having a real home and a family—something she had never had.

When Theresa opened the bedroom door she found Pike slumped on the couch, a game controller twisting in his hands as creatures' heads exploded on the television screen in front of him.

"Still pushing back the boundaries of scientific research?" she asked.

Pike cackled and shot another alien. His backpack lay on the seat beside him.

"Where have you been?" she asked. "Tone's been looking for you. He's really pissed."

"Sorry, sorry," Pike said. "Partied too much last night. Phone's been dead for hours." The screen announced that he'd just died. "Shit," he said and dropped the controller. He looked up at Theresa. "So what's getting up your tight-assed boyfriend's nose this morning?"

"You wouldn't say that to his face," Theresa said. "You'd never get another passing grade."

"True enough. Where is he anyway?"

"He got an email this morning saying he got the big research fellowship he was after. Seeger's making a big deal of it at the department meeting at ten. The press is going to be there—the whole works."

"So Seeger's playing the he-owes-everything-he-is-to-my-wonderful-department card. You going?"

"I can't. Allen's called a drama meeting for the same time. He's got something in the works, and I think he's going to cast me in a major role." Her eyes gleamed with excitement. "This could be a break for me. Allen's getting quite a reputation in the theater scene, so everyone who's anyone will be there. If I do a good job, I'll be noticed. I know it's only being noticed in Ashford, but it's a start."

"Hey, we've all got to start somewhere," Pike said. "But Tone must have loved it when you told him you couldn't come."

"He wasn't happy. Can you be there this morning? He wants you there, and it might take some of the pressure off me."

"Sure." Pike shrugged. "I've got to go there anyway to hand in my assignment."

"*Your* assignment?"

Pike grinned. "It's kind of a collaborative effort. All I need to do now is remember where it is." He hauled himself to his feet and looked vaguely around the room.

"Can you give me a ride in? I don't want to be late for my meeting."

"Yeah." Pike sounded distracted. He picked up his backpack and stared over at Tone's desk. "Give me a minute to dig out my assignment. I'll see you in the car."

"Okay, thanks." Theresa grabbed her backpack and headed outside. She tilted her head up and closed her eyes to appreciate the morning sun on her face. Its warmth drained her anger at Tone and left space for her to look forward to her meeting.

For weeks it had been obvious that Allen was working on something big and that he wanted Theresa to be a part of it. But what was it? And what role was he going to give her?

She hoped his new work wasn't too experimental. Theresa preferred more traditional dramas that concentrated on people and how they dealt with the problems thrown at them by the real world.

She took in a breath of fresh air and listened to the birds. The suburbs were boring—far too boring for Pike, she knew—but they were peaceful. She opened her eyes and stared at his souped-up red WRX, parked at an angle across the driveway. It looked totally out of place on this quiet, tree-lined street of bungalows.

Theresa nodded to the old guy from two doors down who was out walking his equally aged dog. The man smiled back. "Another beautiful day," he commented.

"Lovely day for a stroll," she agreed. She opened the passenger door and grimaced. Pike was obsessed about the outside of his car and how smoothly the engine ran, but he treated the inside like a garbage dump. She brushed crumbs off the black-leather bucket seat, shoved the chip packets and candy wrappers to one side and climbed in. The garbage crackled loudly as she dropped her backpack beside her feet.

Pike stepped out of the house, locked the front door and opened the WRX's hatch with the remote. He put in his backpack and closed it.

"Afraid you'll lose your pack if you put it inside the car?" she asked.

"Ha-ha."

The car shot out of the driveway, and the tires squealed as Pike aimed it down the road.

"I wish I had the contract to supply you with new tires," Theresa remarked.

"The deal was, I give you a ride to the university. There was nothing about snide comments about my car or the way I drive."

"Okay, sorry."

"If Tone's going to MIT, are you going with him?"

"Why wouldn't I?"

"No reason, really. It's just I've sensed some tension between you two lately."

Theresa looked at Pike, surprised he had noticed anything between his partying and his video games.

"It's nothing. Tone's just been stressed. It'll blow over."

"Hmm. MIT's in Boston, right?"

"Cambridge. Just across the river."

"Okay, but don't they get, like, six feet of snow a year?"

"Four feet, on average," Theresa corrected. "Although they can get a lot more in a bad year."

"By any sane person's definition, four feet of snow's a bad year. Didn't you want to go to California—the sunshine and the beach?"

"The fellowship comes with six months a year at some research place in California."

Pike pulled into the university parking lot. "Better hope it's October to March." He parked, and they headed across campus.

As they walked, Pike looked up at the gray, square monolith that was the physics building. "You know why I hardly ever come here?"

"Because you're lazy and you'd rather be partying or sleeping?" Theresa suggested with a smile.

"Yeah, well, partly," he admitted with a laugh. Then his voice lost the light tone that always made Theresa doubt he was saying anything important. "But mainly I feel depressed every time I come here. That building"—he pointed at the physics building—"feels like a prison. It sucks me in and drains all my energy." Pike chewed his lip before continuing. "You know how I learned English?"

Theresa shook her head.

"From pirated DVDs and CDs. I've seen every crap American movie released in the last ten years, most of them ten times, and I know every word of every Beyoncé song. I fell for the American dream—you know, anything's possible through hard work, equal opportunity for all, et cetera, et cetera. When my dad said I could come and study here, I was thrilled."

"But the condition was that you study physics?"

"Yeah. I got my dream, but it turned out to be a nightmare." He rubbed his hand across the back of his neck. "You know what I do sometimes?"

She shook her head.

"I skip lectures. No, don't laugh," he added quickly as Theresa's eyebrows rose. "I skip lectures and go to the library. I hide out in the Asian Studies section and read history books."

"What kind of history books?"

"Anything, really. Like you, I was taught Chinese history in school. I loved it—all the stories about emperors and wars and such—but I wanted to know more. I wanted to know more about what other countries, particularly the United States, thought about China, and I wanted to learn about places like India, Korea, Vietnam. Even Japan."

"So you're turning into an historian!" Theresa exclaimed, genuinely impressed.

"I can't. As long as my dad's paying, I have to do what he wants me to do."

Pike fell silent, and Theresa couldn't think of anything to say. They walked for a bit before he suddenly grinned and spoke again.

"You know, sometimes I just think, Fuck all this stress. I'll get in the car and point it west—see where it takes me." He cast her a sideways glance. "Come with me."

Theresa laughed out loud. "A fast car and a road trip into the setting sun? Thanks for the offer, Pike, but I graciously decline."

"Probably smart. I've got plenty of money in the bank, but the way I spend it, we'd be broke by Denver. Look, today's a big day for Tone. You definitely not coming to the announcement?"

"Don't you start."

"Sorry." Pike held up his hands. "I'm just saying. You know Tone."

"Better than anyone, and I'm thrilled that he got this. But it's a big day for me too."

"Well, are we going to the Blue Bar later to celebrate?"

"Maybe. Tone said something about it."

"I'll give you a full report on how Seeger hijacks Tone's moment and credits the department with everything," Pike said. "Good luck getting the part you want. Let me know if there're any good sex scenes in the play."

Theresa laughed again. "Pike, you're hopeless."

"I know," he agreed, "but I hide it behind a veneer of charm and wit."

"You believe what you want"—Theresa glanced at her watch—"but charm and wit won't do you much good if you're late for Tone's meeting. And I've got to hurry too."

As Theresa headed off toward the theater, Pike called after her, "See you at the Blue Bar tonight."

He got no reply.

CHAPTER THREE

Nanjing, Jiangsu

Night, December 13–14, 1937

"Where are you going?" Lily asks Hill as she comes up behind him. He's already outside the university on the devastated streets close to the boundary of the Safety Zone by the time she catches him. "You need to rest."

The sun has set, but the light from the many fires is reflected off the low clouds, bathing the city in an unearthly reddish glow. The irregular clatter of small-arms fire is interspersed with louder explosions.

Hill is concentrating on keeping to the deeper shadows and starts at Lily's voice. "I'm not ready to rest," he says, turning to face her. "What are *you* doing here?"

He looks so uncomfortable that Lily ignores his question. "You're not leaving the Safety Zone, are you?"

"I have to. Please just go back." Hill looks around nervously.

"Why do you have to leave? Your father's safe in here now."

"Please, Lily, just forget that you saw me."

"I can't, Hill."

The two stand staring at each other in the gloom. Hill knows it's wrong to do what he plans to do without telling Lily and Neil. He had intended to tell them, but Peterson annoyed him with all his talk of safety. Didn't he realize no one was safe anymore?

Hill sighs. "Okay, I'll tell you. But you must promise not to say anything to anyone else."

"All right," she says hesitantly.

Hill sits on a piece of broken masonry. Lily stands beside him.

"I have a brother, Chen," he says.

"You've never mentioned him before."

"I barely know him. He's five years older than me. I was only twelve when he left home to join the army after the Mukden Incident. We were living in Shanghai. My mother had died the year before, and Father begged him to stay to keep the family together. But Chen was determined—he hated the Japanese and swore to help drive them out of Manchuria. Father hardly ever talked about him once he'd left, and he became angry when I asked questions."

Lily sits on the concrete beside Hill, who looks at her with a wistful half smile.

"Chen was my hero growing up. He was the perfect big brother—he taught me things, took me to plays when traveling theaters came to town, protected me when bigger kids threatened me. I was devastated when he went off to war, but I admired him. He wrote no letters home, so Father and I had no idea what he was doing. But I was certain he was a hero. I would lie in bed at night making up stories about how he was bravely fighting against the Japanese, how he would drive them out of our land on his own. Whenever the Japanese demanded more and our government gave in or our soldiers surrendered, I imagined it was because Chen wasn't there. I pictured him as Lord Guan from the play Peterson's putting on—someone who never failed, who could control destiny and was unbeatable in battle.

"As I got older, I realized how childish and naïve my idolization of Chen was, but I couldn't entirely escape it. Even as my image of him as the crusading warrior out to free our land faded, another took its place. I began to see Chen as someone who had escaped the dull life I was destined to live in my father's house. I was determined to learn and prepare myself for my own escape. I began to hang around the International Settlement, doing odd jobs. Mostly I worked for British families, and some of them took time to teach me English.

"It was in Shanghai that I met Shimada. He encouraged my interest in theater and introduced me to Noh, Kabuki and even puppet theater—Bunraku. At first I resisted. After all, Chen was somewhere in the north fighting the Japanese. But Shimada was generous and kind, and he convinced me that not all Japanese are evil. He encouraged me to consider studying in Kyoto, and I saw this as a way to escape. Once in Japan,

I could then go elsewhere. When Shimada came here to Nanjing, I came with him."

Hill laughs nervously. He's never told anyone about his past or his private thoughts, but now that he's begun, he can't stop.

"Anyway, in August, after the fighting broke out in Shanghai, Chen appeared at Father's house. He was a lieutenant and part of the army sent to drive the Japanese out of Shanghai. Father had convinced himself that Chen was dead, so it was a tremendous shock to see him. Chen didn't stay long—and he said nothing about his life in those missing years—but all through the fighting around Shanghai, he sent Father short notes letting him know that he was still alive. When the battle was lost, he turned up again at Father's house and persuaded him to leave and come to Nanjing. On the way, they picked up other refugees and wounded or lost soldiers. Chen organized those who were armed and fit enough into a squad to protect the others."

"Chen was with your father on the road?" Lily asks.

"Yes," Hill says. "But he wasn't there when the Japanese patrol found them. He'd taken his group off to a nearby village to forage for food. All the wounded soldiers and male civilians were dead by the time they returned. Father told me that my brother was devastated and blamed himself for not being there to protect everyone. Some of the men wanted to go after the Japanese patrol and kill them, but Chen said no. He said everyone had to stay together from that point on."

"And he's in Nanjing now?"

Hill nods.

"Why didn't he come into the Safety Zone with your father?"

"Father said Chen doesn't believe the Safety Zone is actually safe. He thinks it's just something set up by foreigners to draw soldiers in so they can be handed over to the Japanese. But I think Chen told Father that because he plans to stay outside the zone and keep on fighting the Japanese."

"And you're going to find him and join him?"

Hill stares at her for a long time. "Find him, yes," he says. "Chen and I fighting the Japanese side by side would be the realization of my childhood dream. But I know the battle's lost. Will I join him and share whatever fate destiny holds for him?" Hill lets the question hang. "Now, Lily, I must go, and you must return to the university."

The two stand up.

"How will you find him?" Lily asks.

"My father didn't want me to do this—he said I would be disappointed—but he did tell me he had left Chen in a warehouse near the Taiping Gate. He was still hiding there last night, but there was a lot of fighting in that area of the city today."

"Be careful," she says, embracing him.

Hill watches as she turns away and heads back toward the university. The temptation to follow her is almost overwhelming.

When Hill crosses Chungyang Road, he leaves the Safety Zone. The first thing he notices is that the level of destruction is much greater here than around the university. Several recently bombed buildings are still burning, and rubble from collapsed walls spreads over the roads. The bodies of Chinese soldiers and civilians lie scattered everywhere, many half buried in the rubble. Hill progresses with caution, dashing between patches of cover and staring at open areas for long minutes before venturing out.

As he nears the Taiping Gate the sound of scattered small-arms fire increases, as does the number of bodies lying in the open. He hears a woman's scream and coarse male laughter coming from a ruined building. On three occasions he hides behind piles of rubble as squads of Japanese soldiers pass by. On the last they are so close that Hill is convinced they'll hear his pounding heart.

When he can no longer hear the soldiers' boots, he rises, looks carefully around and darts across the road into a large building whose half-demolished walls rise to a considerable height. Some interior walls still support the floor above, which appears mostly sound, although it has collapsed in places. The ground is littered with burned beams, some of which are still warm to the touch, and broken furniture. The darkness is almost total, and Hill can only stumble around, banging his shins painfully against fallen objects. Each time he does, he holds his breath and waits to hear if there is any response to the noise. Eventually he finds himself in the corner of the room and slides down onto the floor, shaking with nervous exhaustion.

He must be close to where Chen was last night, but even if he's still here, it will prove more difficult to find him than Hill had first thought. The devastation is worse than he expected, and even in the night there are many Japanese soldiers about. Some appear to be on formal patrols, but others are drunk and simply on the lookout for something to steal or someone to rape.

Hill huddles down. He wonders now if he was insane to come here. On impulse he came to find his hero brother and perhaps even fight alongside him, but he has no weapon, no military training and no courage. Worst of all, Chen is probably miles away. It's obvious that the Battle of Nanjing is lost, so why would Chen stay? He probably came here only to protect their father, and now he has taken his soldiers back out into the countryside to fight the Japanese. Hill feels stupid. Now he'll have to work his way back to the Safety Zone. Somehow that seems a much more difficult and dangerous journey than the one here.

Waves of exhaustion sweep over him. The possibility of seeing Chen again—a wish of Hill's for so many years—has clearly swamped his sanity. The wish kept him going, but now reality is overwhelming the dream, and fear is choking him. Hill is alone in a ruined building surrounded by soldiers who will shoot him as soon as he shows himself. He closes his eyes. Perhaps if he rests for ten minutes he will calm down.

The next thing Hill hears is the sound of nearby voices. At first he's confused—where is he?—and then he panics. The Japanese have found him, and he's going to be shot or bayoneted to death. But why are the voices speaking Chinese?

He remains completely still. He can see a pale light stuttering in the next room. There's a thump and a shout of pain, followed by another voice ordering quiet. Hill relaxes a bit—people speaking Chinese and stumbling in the dark can't be too dangerous.

The light appears in the doorway. It's a flashlight, pointed at the ground and shielded by a man's hand. There are several shadowy figures behind it.

The man holding the flashlight moves into the room. He's leading the others toward the door out to the street. Inexplicably, he hesitates. The flashlight beam begins a long, slow sweep of the room. Hill holds his breath and makes himself as small as possible. The beam sweeps over him, but then it returns and settles on his face.

Hill hears the sound of a rifle bolt being drawn back.

"Don't shoot," he says.

"Who are you?" a voice asks.

"My name is Hill Chao," he manages to croak out.

There's a long pause. "What are you doing here?"

"I've come from the Safety Zone," he says. "I'm looking for my brother."

The figure with the flashlight steps forward. "Stand up," the voice orders.

Hill stands. The light shines harshly in his face, and Hill knows the man is examining him.

"What makes you think your brother is here?"

"He came into Nanjing three days ago with my father. My father made it into the Safety Zone yesterday and told me he had last seen my brother near the Taiping Gate. That's why I came to look for him here."

There's another long silence, and then the man shines the flashlight up on his own face. It takes a minute for Hill's eyes to adjust, and at first he thinks he's looking at an old man. The face is thin, unshaven, filthy and heavily lined. The cheeks are hollow, and the deep-set eyes red-rimmed. Gradually Hill begins to see past the dirt and the weariness in the eyes to a younger face filled with anger and hope.

"Chen?" he asks.

The figure nods slowly, as if the effort of acknowledging his identity is almost too much.

Hill steps forward and opens his arms to embrace his brother, but Chen steps back.

"You should not be here," he says angrily.

Hill stops, confused by the rejection. "I came searching for you." On impulse he adds, "I want to fight by your side, with your squad."

Chen laughs—a harsh, cruel sound. "You always were naïve. You buried your nose in books and ignored the world around you. What do you know about fighting? I've been fighting in the real world for six years. Everyone I know is dead. I've seen friends shot, blown up and burned to death beside me. I've done things I hope you never even have to imagine, and I lie awake in terror most nights." Chen swings his flashlight in an arc over the other soldiers in the room. "These are my noble warriors."

As near as Hill can tell, there are about a dozen men, all dirty and dressed in tattered uniforms. Some have filthy, blood-encrusted rags wrapped around their heads or faces. Two men have arms in makeshift slings, and one is leaning on crutches made from broken pieces of wood. Most have rifles either pointing at Hill or slung over their shoulders, and all look exhausted and stare back with dumb, empty eyes.

"Four months ago we went into Shanghai," Chen says. "We were part of the 88th Division, proud to be the elite unit in our army. We had been trained by the Germans. We almost drove the Japanese Marines out of the city, but when they landed north of Shanghai we were lost. They had more planes, artillery and tanks, and their battleships were anchored offshore, throwing huge shells in among our troops.

"We fought for almost three months in the streets around the Northern Railway Station. It was like living in hell. Our men would strap explosives to their bodies and throw themselves under Japanese tanks, but it was no use. We were defeated, and those left alive were ordered to Nanjing to fight. I went to Shanghai with a battalion of four hundred men—this is what's left." Chen waves his arm around the room. "It's finished. You're welcome to come and die with us if you wish."

The harshness in Chen's tone hurts Hill. "What...what are you going to do?" he stammers.

"We're going to find some Japanese to kill before they kill us."

"That's suicide."

Again, Chen's brutal laugh. "This war *is* suicide. We cannot beat the Japanese. They're too strong, they have better weapons and better training, and our best soldiers are rotting in mass graves around Shanghai. We have only two decisions left: we can surrender and be shot, beheaded or used for bayonet practice, or we can try to take a few of them with us."

Hill is shocked by his brother's bleak, hopeless view. What has happened to the hero he imagined? Can the horrors his brother described really have happened? But after what his father told him, Hill knows in his heart they can. Maybe Chen is right. Maybe death *is* inevitable.

Then an idea comes to him. "There is a third choice," he blurts.

Chen smirks at him. "What choice can you offer dead men?"

"I can take you to the Safety Zone."

"The Safety Zone is a lie."

"No, it's not," Hill says passionately. "I've come from there. It was set up by some foreigners to protect refugees. The Japanese have agreed that people in the Safety Zone will be safe. There's a hospital there, so your men's wounds can be treated."

"The Japanese won't allow soldiers in."

Chen sounds firm, but Hill sees a glimmer of uncertainty in his eyes.

"There are more than two hundred thousand refugees in the Safety Zone," he declares. "We can give you civilian clothing and hide you. You'll be safe."

"You want us to hide among the women and children?"

"It's the only chance you have to make other choices. Only someone alive can make a decision."

Chen still hesitates.

"Ask *them* if they want to live," Hill says, pointing at the wounded soldiers.

"How would we get to this Safety Zone?"

Hill relaxes. He knows he's persuaded Chen. "It won't be easy, but it's not far, and I know the way. If we're careful and we leave now, we can get there before dawn."

Chen thinks for a long time, then sighs. "All right, little brother. We'll try it your way."

"You'll have to leave the rifles behind," Hill says.

For a moment it seems as though Chen is going to protest, but he just nods. "It makes no difference. We have only two bullets for each gun."

Hill steps forward once more. This time Chen doesn't retreat. The brothers embrace.

CHAPTER FOUR

Ashford, Ohio

Present Day

Pike wandered down the deserted hallway. He stopped at the closed door of room 101 and stared at Professor Kenneth Seeger's nameplate. He knocked. There was no response. Good timing, Pike thought, as he dug the assignment out of his backpack and put it in the tray beside the door. He really wasn't in the mood for one of Seeger's lectures on how close he was to flunking out. This was a big assignment, worth 25 percent of the course. A good mark would pull him up a few grade points and remove some of the pressure to do well in the term-ending exam.

He continued on to the lecture hall where the department meeting was about to begin. A few latecomers were hustling through the door, and Pike joined them. Inside, the hall was almost full. Pike spotted the back of Tone's head in the center of the front row. There was an empty seat on either side of him.

As Pike debated whether he wanted to attract attention to himself by going down to the front, Tone twisted around and noticed him. Pike waved and gestured to a nearby empty seat. Tone looked nervous but smiled and nodded as his friend sat down and placed his backpack on the floor between his feet. The buzz of conversation died as Professor Seeger strode in through a side door and positioned himself behind the lectern in front of a Smart Board.

Seeger was a short man, pushing sixty, Pike guessed. He moved quickly, seemed to do everything abruptly and affected a mock cheerfulness that Pike hated. Despite his Midwestern accent, he'd adopted a faux-British manner, wearing tweed jackets and sporting half-moon reading glasses and colorful bow ties.

Seeger stood at the lectern for a moment, savoring the audience before him. Then he brought the flat of his hand down sharply. He smiled and repeated the gesture. As he slowly increased the tempo, the audience picked it up, slapping the folding tables attached to the arms of their chairs or stamping their feet in time with him, and soon there was a deafening crescendo of noise.

Seeger stopped suddenly and held up his hands. "Welcome, everyone," he said when the silence was complete. "Thank you for coming this morning to this special departmental meeting."

A camera flashed to one side, and Pike noticed the reporter and photographer from the *Ashford Star*.

"Physics is often considered a dry subject," Seeger said, addressing his remarks to the reporter, who dutifully began taking notes. "Dry and not very much fun." He paused to scan the room. "I have to tell you that this morning, I *am* having fun."

There were a few forced chuckles from the front rows.

"Eastern University is a small school, and the physics department is often viewed—unfairly, I must point out—as a poor relative of the drama and humanities departments. But it *is* true that we cannot hope to match the research resources of the large Ivy League universities—a Higgs boson discovery is not for us."

A small but knowing chuckle ran through the audience, and the reporter furrowed his brow in confusion. Seeger held up his hand for silence, even though what laughter there had been had already subsided.

"But we can produce some damned fine students who will go on to bigger and grander things elsewhere." Seeger stared over his glasses at Tone, who shifted uncomfortably in his seat. "We have with us this morning one such student. Tone, will you come forward and join me?"

Tone hesitated but rose and moved beside Seeger. As he turned to face the audience, he looked at Pike, who smiled and gave him a thumbs-up.

"Tone Zhang is the reason I am having so much fun this morning," Seeger said, placing a hand on Tone's shoulder. "Since arriving from China, Tone has contributed greatly to this department. His theoretical work in the field of cryogenics is groundbreaking and, I am certain, in the future will revolutionize this field of our discipline.

"Every generation of scientists surpasses the one before it. As Isaac Newton said, 'If I have seen further, it is by standing upon the shoulders of giants.' I do not consider myself a giant. However, as a tutor and mentor, I must confess to feeling the weight of Tone's feet on my shoulders."

There was more laughter this time. Even Pike joined in—although he was laughing not at Seeger's weak joke but at what he knew must be going through Tone's head. Tone had never made any secret of the fact that he considered Seeger a pompous windbag who had never and would never contribute an original thought to his science.

"With great pleasure and not a little pride, I announce to you all that this morning we learned Tone Zhang has been awarded the prestigious Kelvin Fellowship in Low-Temperature Research at MIT."

This time the applause was genuine. There were even a few whistles, and a scattering of people stood. Tone smiled uneasily as Seeger patted him on the back and shook his hand. The reporter's camera flashed.

As the applause died away and people settled back down, Seeger whispered something in Tone's ear and pushed him forward. Tone hesitated, and Pike noticed that his fists were clenched.

"Thank you," Tone began when he took the mic. "I have enjoyed my time here at Eastern."

Seeger beamed.

Tone cleared his throat and scanned the audience rapidly. As the pause lengthened the people sitting near Pike shifted restlessly. A line of worry creased Seeger's forehead.

Pike was surprised that Tone was so nervous. He had seen him present scientific papers without any sign of stress. Then again, this was different, he supposed. With a scientific paper on work Tone knew like the back of his hand, he was in control. In a situation like this, where he was expected to be spontaneous, the control was with the audience—and with Seeger.

"Professor Seeger is correct," Tone said tentatively. "All new research owes a debt to the work of those who have gone before. In the field of cryogenics, the shoulders upon which I stand began with Zimri-Lim, the Mari ruler who ordered the first icehouses to be constructed on the banks of the Euphrates almost four thousand years ago."

As he talked, Tone visibly relaxed. "Over the centuries many other great minds have contributed to my field of research: Boyle, Avogadro, Faraday, Wróblewski, von Linde, Onnes..."

Tone continued with his long list of names—most of which meant nothing to Pike or, judging by the increasingly restless noises, many of those seated around him.

"More recently, and more directly related to my work..."

Pike noticed that Seeger was smiling again, no doubt expecting his name to appear in the august company of Tone's next list.

"The discovery—by Kapitsa, Allen and Misener—of superfluidity in the 1930s was a seminal moment in cryogenics and provided the shoulders upon which Lee, Richardson and Osheroff stood when they discovered the superfluidity of helium-3 at 0.002 degrees Kelvin. That in turn allowed Cornell and Wieman to create the very first Bose-Einstein condensate. Just recently, in the lab at my soon-to-be home, MIT, they cooled sodium potassium gas to five hundred nanokelvins."

Tone scanned the room, expecting a reaction. He got nothing. Seeger's smile looked increasingly strained.

Tone tried again. "That's about 450 degrees Fahrenheit colder than it gets here in winter."

"Jesus, Tone. Don't tell your joke," Pike hissed under his breath.

"Have you heard about the man who was cooled to absolute zero?"

Pike groaned so loudly that his neighbor glanced at him.

Tone smiled and delivered the punch line: "He's OK now."

Two people in the audience sniggered.

"OK," Tone said, "is shorthand for zero degrees Kelvin—absolute zero."

Even the audience members who understood what he'd been talking about didn't laugh. Tone looked like he was dying. Pike knew what was coming next. When his friend felt threatened, his natural defense was arrogance.

"I guess I'll stay away from standup comedy." He straightened up, and his gaze became more assured. "My recent paper in the *Journal of Low Temperature Physics*, which some of you may have read"—Tone managed to sound supremely condescending—"is the summit of the column of shoulders I have mentioned. I'm certain that, using the fantastic resources available at MIT and in conjunction with the extraordinary academic minds that grace the department there, my research will blossom and I'll be able to see further in the field of cryogenics than anyone before me. Thank you." Tone gave a halfhearted grin and returned to his seat in the front row.

There was a moment of deafening silence, and then Pike began clapping. Gradually others joined in, and the room filled with polite applause. Seeger stepped forward, obviously struggling to hide his displeasure.

He wants to beat the shit out of Tone, Pike thought.

"Thank you, Tone," the professor said in a monotone. "I'm certain that those below you will feel the weight of your research." He turned back to the room. "I'm also certain," he said in a lighter voice, "that most of you came to hear the announcement and do not wish to attend the more mundane activities of a departmental meeting." There was an audible sigh of relief. "Therefore, we shall adjourn for ten minutes, after which time all department staff will reconvene in the conference room on the second floor. Thank you."

Tone stood, obviously expecting Seeger to come and talk to him. But the department head had turned away and was talking earnestly to the reporter as he led the man out of the room.

A few people came up, shook Tone's hand and offered congratulations, but most hustled out in search of coffee or toward their next lecture. Tone stood at the front of the room and watched it empty.

"Asshole," he said when he and Pike were the only two left.

"Yeah," Pike said. "I think we're agreed on that."

"He didn't even shake my hand at the end." He sounded genuinely upset.

"Well, you did piss him off."

Tone looked puzzled. "I know it wasn't the smoothest presentation I've ever given, but I was nervous. I didn't say anything that isn't true."

"Maybe, but you also didn't say what Seeger wanted to hear."

"I said I'd enjoyed my time at Eastern."

"But you never mentioned Seeger once. You listed everyone, going back thousands of years, except Seeger."

"But he's not a major figure in cryogenics."

"He's your supervisor."

"All he's done is supervise. Every word of my thesis—every original idea in there—is mine. The man's an idiot."

"I know," Pike said as he and Tone headed for the back door, "but you could have been a bit more diplomatic."

"You're saying I should lie to get Seeger to like me?"

"I'm saying you need to learn to play the game, Tone."

"I don't like games," Tone said, slamming the door behind them. "My work is what's important. That's what I'll be remembered for long after Seeger's a drooling idiot in a home somewhere."

Pike decided not to pursue the conversation—it could only further inflame Tone's defensive anger. They walked along the corridor in silence. It was Tone who finally broke it.

"Did you see Theresa this morning?" he asked.

"Yeah," Pike said, relieved to be on safer conversational ground. "She was still at the house when I got back. I gave her a ride here."

"To go to her dumb drama meeting?"

"Give her a break, Tone. It's a big thing for her." Pike wanted to point out that Tone's meeting hadn't gone spectacularly well, but he kept his mouth shut. "Anyway, congratulations, man. That's awesome news about the MIT thing."

"Thanks, Pike." Tone brightened. "It's like a new beginning. At least, it will be as soon as I get away from this shitty little school and that pompous prick Seeger." He stopped in the middle of the corridor. "Were you at Harry's last night?"

"Indeed I was," Pike said, a broad grin spreading across his puffy face.

"Did you get it?" Tone glanced both ways down the corridor. It was empty.

Pike crouched, unzipped his backpack and rummaged deep into it. He pulled up the revolver and held it just below the open zipper. There was a red bow tied around the barrel.

"You got a revolver," Tone said as he stared at the snub-nosed weapon.

"Yeah," Pike said. "Ruger SP101—five rounds, .357 magnum, double-action."

"The bow's a nice touch," Tone said, reaching for the gun.

Pike pushed the revolver back into the bag. "Not here, man. I'll take you out to the range tomorrow and show you how it works. I've got a full box of ammo. You can blow the shit out of as many targets as you like." Something in the eagerness in Tone's face worried him. "You sure you want this?"

"Of course. For as long as I can remember, I've wanted a gun. When I get my own place, I'm going to start a collection. This'll be number one. This country's a great place to do that."

"Living the American dream."

The sarcasm was lost on Tone. "Yeah. You've got your fast car, and now I've got my gun."

"It's not cheap," Pike said. "A thousand even for the gun and the ammo. You could have saved a few hundred going down to Walmart."

"The money doesn't matter. I just didn't want the hassle of the background check."

"Okay."

Pike zipped up his backpack and swung it over his shoulder. "I'm going back to the house this afternoon to catch some sleep—I didn't get a lot last night. We going to the Blue Bar tonight?"

"Of course. Theresa's coming, and then I'm going to take her for a nice meal at that expensive Italian place."

"Cool. I'll see you then." Pike headed round the corner of the building.

Tone watched him go and then set off in the direction of the theater.

The Neil Peterson Memorial Theater held an audience of 250 in three sections of steeply tiered seats. When the theater was full, the intimidating impression from the small stage was of performing in front of a wall of people. This morning most of the seats were empty, with only a few at the front occupied by lounging drama students. Other students stood around in small groups talking. When Theresa entered by the top door and walked down the side aisle, she felt surrounded by a low mumble carried up by the room's impressive acoustics.

She had covered half the distance to the stage when a figure stepped out from the curtains on one side. Allen Quigley was tall and slim, with long fair hair tied in a ponytail that swished from side to side as he scanned the room. His gray eyes sparkled with enthusiasm, and his mouth was curled in a smile.

"Good morning, thespians and dramatists," he said as he reached the front of the stage. When he saw Theresa coming down the stairs his smile broadened. "I'm so happy you came." He turned his attention back to the other students. "I'm glad all of you came."

Theresa felt strangely restless as she reached the bottom of the steps. It was as if the room had an energy that wouldn't let her relax. Nodding to a couple of friends, she leaned against the wall at the side of the stage.

Most of the chatting actors found themselves seats, and when everyone was settled Quigley composed his face into a more serious expression and addressed them.

"As you are all aware, this theater is named for Neil Peterson, Eastern University's most famous drama graduate. His will provided the funds for the theater's construction, and so, in a very real sense, everything we do on this stage is a part of Peterson's legacy to the world of drama. What some of you may not know is that next month marks both the one hundred and seventh anniversary of Peterson's birth and the fiftieth of his death. I think this is an occasion worth celebrating, so I've obtained permission from the university to stage a play in Peterson's honor."

"Please, Allen," implored a student lounging in the front row, "don't say it's going to be *The Black Circus*. That play's been done to death by every drama class and club in the country."

"And justifiably, Gord," Quigley retorted. "It *is* Peterson's masterpiece—and one of the great plays of the twentieth century."

An audible groan ran through the assembled students. Quigley held up his hands in mock surrender.

"Relax, relax! *The Black Circus* is not the play we're going to do."

"What then?" Gord asked. "Peterson wasn't prolific, and most critics agree that his early plays are poorly developed, that he didn't begin to fulfill his potential until after his time in the Second World War. Even then, his work is like a trial run for the themes in *The Black Circus*—love, loneliness, the past. If we do one of his early plays, we'll only be inviting unfavorable comparisons with his masterpiece."

"You're correct," Quigley said, smiling down at the student. "The Second World War—and Peterson's experience of it—is generally acknowledged to be the prime influence on his work. And yes, that influence reached stunning fruition in *The Black Circus*, and almost everything else he wrote cannot compare to it."

"*Almost* everything else he wrote?" Theresa said from the shadows.

"Well spotted." Allen looked over at her. He held the stare and silence a moment longer than necessary, then looked back at the audience. "But we'll get to that in a moment. First some background."

Quigley moved forward and sat on the edge of the stage. "Peterson studied at Eastern in the early thirties and wrote a few frankly juvenile plays. In the summer of 1937 he went to China to study the thirteenth-century plays of Guan Hanqing, the playwright whose work Peterson had researched for his postgraduate degree here. He was there for only a few months, and as far as we know, he never published anything about those times—although he was there during the first months of the war with Japan. When he returned to America, he became a recluse, living in near poverty in New York, and we know from comments he made later and from surviving rough drafts that he attempted to write a play set in China. He never completed it.

"In 1942 Peterson volunteered for the navy. He served throughout the war years in the information department, writing short propaganda plays and entertainments for the troops. He never saw action, although he applied to be sent on active service several times. Apparently, he had flat feet." Quigley shrugged dramatically.

"Although Peterson never published anything of significance during the war, there is strong evidence that he continued to work on his unfinished Chinese play. After the war he lived outside Los Angeles for several years. His plays from those years began to gain notice and critical acclaim, and they all show, in some form, the ideas that came together so well in *The Black Circus*. Peterson's ideas were no doubt influenced by his reading of Jean-Paul Sartre. Interestingly, there is some evidence that Peterson met Sartre on a trip to Europe in 1957."

Quigley slid down off the stage and began pacing back and forth in front of the seats. "Oh, to have been a fly on the wall during that conversation! Did the two great men discuss the idea that our morality can be defined only by the choices we make? That we can only make choices because we are free, yet every choice we make limits our freedom?"

He stopped pacing and stared at Theresa. She had the strong impression that he was seeing Peterson and Sartre deep in conversation in a café in Montparnasse.

"We know all this," Gord complained, interrupting Quigley's reverie. "We did a section on Peterson last semester. You were the TA for it."

"Apologies for the digression—and for boring you, Gord. Unfortunately, not everyone is as well informed as you. But I'm almost done!" Quigley snapped his head up and returned to his pacing. "Toward the end of the war Peterson made a concerted attempt to rework the fragments of his Chinese play. He managed to complete two acts of what one must suppose was intended to be a three-act piece. It is by no means as polished, sophisticated or complex as his later work, but the two completed acts do have a raw power to them. The frequency with which Peterson returned to his Chinese play suggests it was very important to him—and that poses the question: Why could he not complete the third act?"

"Are you proposing we put on an unfinished piece of Peterson's work?" Gord asked. He was sitting up now, paying close attention. "And one that you yourself admitted is not polished, sophisticated or complex?"

"I'm afraid you missed something I mentioned earlier," Quigley said. "I said we were going to put on a play, not that we were going to put on one of *Peterson's* plays."

"What?!" Gord said.

Most of the students looked totally confused. But in a blinding flash Theresa realized what Allen was going to say. She pushed herself off the wall and stepped toward him.

Quigley spoke only to her. "I have written the third act of Peterson's incomplete Chinese play. *That* is what we'll perform."

The announcement was met with silence as the implications sank in. Then Gord swore under his breath. A buzz of conversation broke out.

"Are we going to do a three-act play," Gord asked above the noise, "with two acts by Peterson and one by you?"

"One day, perhaps, that may happen. But we have neither the time nor the resources to stage such an ambitious project. Yes, I have completed Peterson's play, but in such a way that the third act can work as a stand-alone piece." As more murmuring broke out, Quigley held up his hands for silence. "There are a number of meaty roles in my play, and I will post a provisional cast list this afternoon. Those of you with roles can pick up a copy of the play at my office. Time is tight, so we'll begin rehearsals tomorrow with a first read-through. Thank you."

The conversation resumed as the students stood and made for the exits.

"Theresa, could you stay for a moment?" Quigley asked.

When the theater was empty, she spoke first. "Good God, Allen! What made you think you could finish Peterson's play?"

Quigley smiled. "I've never fully subscribed to the notion that Peterson's experiences in the Second World War were the root of his genius. As far as we can tell, he wasn't involved in anything dangerous or dramatic. He wrote propaganda in an office in San Diego, and the only creative work from this time is the unfinished Chinese play. I began to think that the key to Peterson is his experience in China."

"But we know so little about that time," Theresa pointed out.

"Well, that's not strictly true." Quigley pursed his lips. "He kept no diary or journal in China, but he did jot down notes on scraps of paper that are scattered through the boxes of documents he donated to the university shortly before he died. None of the scraps mean very much on their own, but I spent a good part of last summer collecting and collating every reference Peterson made to his time in China."

"That must have taken—" Theresa stopped, unable to find a word to express the magnitude of the task.

Quigley laughed. "Yes, I spent many long, lonely nights in the archives. But it was worth it. If you read all the references to China together, a much more coherent picture emerges. If you then make the assumption—a reasonable one, I think—that the main character in the unfinished play is Peterson himself, it's possible to come up with a picture of what he did in China."

"What? Allen! What did he do?"

Quigley smiled broadly, enjoying the moment. He moved closer to her before he spoke. "The first two acts of Peterson's work are autobiographical. They deal with his decision to go to China, his interest in Guan Hanqing, his arrival at Jinling University in Nanjing and the people he met there. All this is set against a backdrop of rising tensions: the outbreak of war and the Battle of Shanghai. It builds slowly and effectively—and then it stops with the fall of Shanghai in November 1937. We know Peterson was in Nanjing, at the university, when the Japanese attacked the city in December."

"In the Safety Zone."

"I see you've done your homework."

"It's part of my history, Allen. In school we were taught about the Nanjing Massacre, and how John Rabe, along with the foreign doctors and missionaries who had stayed behind when most of the Europeans fled, set up the Safety Zone around the university, as well as several embassies, a hospital and a girls' school. They saved a quarter of a million lives."

"An extraordinary humanitarian achievement," Quigley said, nodding. "And Peterson was a part of it. It must have been nightmarish—that many hungry, terrified people crammed into such a fragile island of safety in a sea of war. The Japanese army all around, slaughtering and raping at will."

The pair stood in silence for a moment, their minds filled with images of horror.

"So why did Peterson stay behind in Nanjing?" Theresa asked at last. "He doesn't strike me as the missionary type."

Quigley leaned in conspiratorially. "He was in love."

"In love! This is incredible. Who was she?"

"Her name was Lily Chan. She was head of the university's drama department, and by all accounts she was stunningly beautiful. There was a third character as well, a Chinese student called Hill Chao. The three of them risked their lives to help Chinese soldiers escape."

"Unbelievable. No one knows about all this! This will be a major contribution to the study of Peterson and his work. You have to publish it."

"I've already written a piece for *Critical Theater* magazine, but I haven't submitted it yet. I want to put this play on first."

"How accurate do you think your third act is?" Theresa asked. "Have you uncovered enough about Peterson's time in China to know what he intended?"

"I think so. Of course, I've had to make leaps of faith sometimes, but we have the advantage of knowing how that experience influenced Peterson's later work. Something that happened in China convinced him that everyone who comes into this world continually faces dilemmas. As individuals we must eternally make choices, but those choices don't solve the problems."

At the back of the theater, the door opened and Tone slipped in. He stood in the shadows, looking down at the two figures deep in conversation in front of the stage. Theresa had her back to him, but Quigley was looking directly at him over her shoulder.

"They simply lead to different dilemmas down the road—but still we must make choices." As he spoke Quigley slowly leaned closer to Theresa. "That's what Peterson saw as the nature of life—of drama—and he developed those ideas in China when he was with Lily."

Theresa could feel Quigley's breath on her cheek. He was almost whispering in her ear. A part of her wanted to draw back, but another part was mesmerized by his words and his closeness.

"I want you to play Lily," Quigley said.

Theresa gasped and flung her arms around Quigley's neck. "Allen, I would love to! To have the chance to be Peterson's muse...thank you. *Thank you.*"

Quigley continued to watch Tone as he returned Theresa's hug. He smiled slightly as Tone turned and slid back out the door.

"You are the embodiment of Lily," he said as he and Theresa drew apart. "You are beautiful, pure and smart, just as Peterson described her. You have presence and grace onstage. You'll be a magnificent Lily...to my Peterson."

"Thank you, Allen." Theresa beamed. "Who will play the part of Hill?"

"I have a radical idea for that. I want someone who contrasts Peterson's intellectualism and Lily's purity and grace. And, of course, someone who is Chinese. I was thinking of your friend Tone."

"Tone!" Theresa looked startled. "Tone's not an actor."

"And that is exactly his strength. In a sense, this is experimental theater. We're doing a fragment of a play that doesn't exist, yet is based on real-world events. The center of my play is the relationship between Peterson and Lily. Hill is peripheral to that, so Tone's main focus will be on reacting to what goes on around him. Besides, like you, he will have learned about the Nanjing Massacre in school. The background will mean something to him. I think it will work. Will you ask him?"

"I'll ask him, but I can't guarantee he'll say yes."

"Fair enough."

"What's your play called?"

Quigley grinned. "Can't you guess?"

Theresa thought for a moment. Then she laughed. "Of course. *The Third Act.*"

CHAPTER FIVE

Nanjing, Jiangsu

Morning, December 14, 1937

"Goddamn it, Hill. What the hell have you done?"

Peterson is standing in the doorway of the cold, windowless basement room of the university. The only light comes from a few guttering candles placed on boxes piled against the walls. Wherever there is a patch of concrete floor among the boxes, a soldier is sitting or lying. Most are asleep despite Peterson's outburst. Chen is standing in the middle of the room, staring at him.

"Where else could I take them?" Hill asks from behind Peterson. "If I'd left them by the Taiping Gate, they'd all be dead by now. And Chen's my brother."

Peterson and Chen stare at each other for a moment. Chen doesn't understand a word that's being said, but he picks up on the tension. Peterson pushes Hill back into the corridor and closes the door behind them.

"Okay, he's your brother—I get that. But why did you have to bring him and the others here? You're putting all our lives at risk. The important thing for all of us right now is to keep a low profile and not antagonize the Japs."

"You want to condemn people to death just so we don't antagonize the Japanese?" Hill's voice rises as his anger increases. "They're murdering people in the streets!"

"And that's exactly why we can't give them an excuse to come here and murder *us*. The Safety Zone is secure only because we stick to the rules that were agreed to with the Japanese—and one of those rules was that we wouldn't allow any soldiers in."

"*Defeated* soldiers!" Hill shouts. "You have no idea what it's like out there. Getting back here was a nightmare. There were patrols and groups of drunken Japanese soldiers everywhere. We spent an hour huddled in a room while soldiers raped and murdered a woman next door." He struggles to control his emotions. "This was the only place I could think of to take Chen and his men. The only place where they would be out of the way." He manages to keep his voice level. "If this were your university back in America, and your town had been attacked by brutal invaders, would you risk your life to rescue your country's soldiers?"

"It's not the same situation," Peterson protests.

"Because these are only Chinese soldiers?"

"No, of course not," Peterson says. "Because there are the lives of a quarter of a million people to consider—almost all of them Chinese."

"And you think the Japanese would slaughter all those people because of the twelve wounded soldiers in this room?"

"No, but they might close the Safety Zone, and then the refugees would be thrown back out in the city to starve."

"Are you certain it's not simply the life of one person you're considering?"

Peterson's eyes narrow. "That's not fair, Hill, and you know it."

Hill shrugs.

"Look," Peterson says, "I agree we can't throw them out in daylight—that would bring the Japanese down on us faster than keeping them here. They can stay for the day, but tonight they have to leave."

He turns and strides down the corridor, leaving Hill glaring at his back. Hill sighs and rubs his eyes. He has barely slept the past two nights. He has to find medical attention for the wounded, and food and civilian clothes for all of them. And now there's the question of what to do tonight when Peterson demands that they leave.

He shakes his head and opens the door. Chen is standing right where he left him.

"Your American friend is not happy with our being here," Chen says.

"No," Hill admits, "but it will work out. Right now I need to find medicine, food and clothing. I'll be back as soon as I can. Stay quiet and don't let anyone leave the room."

Hill sets off, wondering if he's made the wrong decision in bringing Chen here. It's one thing to have young men and boys mixed in with the tens of thousands of women and children in the Safety Zone—the Japanese have no way of knowing which of them are runaway soldiers in civilian clothes. It's quite another thing to bring in a squad of uniformed, wounded soldiers.

Hill curses under his breath. He wishes Chen had stayed in the north, maybe joined the communist army fighting the Japanese there. But there's no point in dwelling on what-ifs. He couldn't leave his brother to die. Faced with the situation at the Taiping Gate again, he would probably make the same decision.

Hill heads first for the backstage costume room to find some clothes—partly because it is the simplest of his tasks and partly because he hopes he'll run into Lily there. Maybe he can persuade her to help him change Peterson's mind about evicting the soldiers.

He sees Lily as soon as he enters the theater, but she's in an intense conversation with Peterson. He feels a surge of jealousy.

"Hill, what have you done?" Lily demands as he moves toward them. "You know we can't take soldiers into the Safety Zone."

"I found my brother," Hill says.

Lily looks stunned. "You *found* him?"

Obviously, Hill thinks, Peterson hasn't got around to telling her that Chen is the leader of the squad. "I did. Chen and eleven soldiers. Most of them wounded, and each with only two bullets left. Chen was about to lead them on a suicide attack on the first Japanese patrol they came across. I couldn't let him die."

"I understand that," Peterson concedes. "But they cannot stay here. Sooner or later the Japanese will find them, and then they'll execute all of us. They have to leave the Safety Zone tonight."

"We can hide them," Hill argues. "I came here to get some clothing for them. We can give them some rice and some medicine. As soon as they're rested, we'll get them out one at a time, so they blend in with the refugee community."

"The Japanese will find them," Peterson insists.

"They won't," Hill says. "There are a quarter of a million refugees in here. How will the Japanese find twelve men?"

"They only need to find one. That'll give them the excuse to come in and do a sweep to find the others. The Safety Zone will be closed, and there'll be a massacre."

"There's a massacre going on already, and the Japanese can come into the Safety Zone any time they like. Who's going to stop them? Can't you hear the gunfire?"

"Of course there's firing," Peterson says defensively. "We're in the middle of a war."

"Doesn't it strike you as odd that we keep hearing bursts of machine-gun fire and most of it is coming from the river? Why do you think that is, Neil? Are they shooting fish?"

Peterson hesitates, overwhelmed by the anger and heavy sarcasm in Hill's voice.

Lily tries to diffuse the situation. "We all agree that even if Chen and the others must go, it would be insanity for everyone if they left the Safety Zone in daylight. So what we do *today* is not going to change. Hill is right—they need clothing, medicine and food. Neil, Hill and I both have contacts at the hospital, so it will be less suspicious if we're the ones to go there. Can you go to the wardrobe department and gather enough clothes for twelve people? Don't pick anything that looks too bright or new. We don't want these men to draw attention to themselves."

For a moment it looks as if Peterson is going to protest, but he merely shrugs and heads backstage.

"Thank you," Hill says as he and Lily cross the campus and head out into the streets of the Safety Zone. A raw wind is blowing from the west, and building clouds threaten snow.

"I'm not supporting you," Lily says, pulling her jacket tighter around her. "It was incredibly stupid of you to bring those men here." Hill opens his mouth to argue, but Lily goes on before he can say anything. "But it was also incredibly brave of you to bring them through the streets at night. If you'd been spotted, the Japanese wouldn't have stopped to ask questions, and Shimada wouldn't have been there to help you."

"I just knew I had to do it. Do you think Neil really would have abandoned them if he'd been in my position?"

"Don't be too hard on him. He comes from a softer culture than ours. He's never had to make life-and-death choices. He may be older than you, but in a way he is much younger."

"I suppose so, but it's hard not to dislike Americans right now. They have the power to stop what's going on here, yet they do nothing. As soon as danger threatens, the American diplomats pack up and flee down the river. Even when one of their ships is bombed, they make a few noises and then everything goes on as usual."

"Don't blame only the Americans. All the other diplomats left as well. And remember, our government was the first to go. Everyone deserted us." Lily suddenly laughs.

"What's so funny?" Hill asks.

"I just realized that the only foreigners who stayed here are a few businessmen, a teacher, a nurse or two and a bunch of missionaries, and they were organized to help us by a Nazi."

"It *is* odd," Hill agrees with a wry smile. "Rabe saved a lot of lives when the bombing was at its worst by spreading those huge Nazi banners all over the place and organizing rice deliveries to the refugees."

"Yes, the Japanese are more afraid of offending Hitler than they are of offending Roosevelt. I wonder what..."

Lily's question trails off as the two come to the large square in front of the imposing bulk of the Catholic cathedral. The square is almost filled with hundreds of refugees being guarded by a platoon of Japanese soldiers. About sixty of the refugees—all men or boys, and several with bloody faces—are being tied together in a group to one side.

"What are the Japanese doing in the Safety Zone?" Lily asks.

"They're rounding up anyone who might be a soldier. We have to go."

Hill and Lily turn to retreat down the side street, but a Japanese soldier blocks their way. He gestures at Hill with the long bayonet on the end of his rifle and asks, "Soldier?"

"No," Hill replies in bad Japanese. "University student." He points in the direction from which they've come.

The Japanese soldier stares thoughtfully at Hill for a moment and then shakes his head. "Soldier," he repeats.

This time it's a statement, not a question.

The soldier grabs Hill by the arm and starts dragging him over to the other men.

"No!" Lily screams, lunging forward. The soldier turns and drives the butt of his rifle into her stomach, forcing all the air out of her body and knocking her to the ground.

Struggling to drag air into her tortured lungs, Lily watches as Hill is tied to the other men and pushed roughly out of the square.

Utter dread sweeps through her.

CHAPTER SIX

Ashford, Ohio

Present Day

The Blue Bar was filled with a small but raucous crowd of students. Green Day thumped from speakers suspended at the corners of the room, and three big-screen TVs displayed various sports events. In a side room a not-very-serious game of pool was under way.

True to its name, everything in the bar was blue: the walls and ceiling, the fake stone bar, the Formica tables and chairs, the felt on the pool table. Behind the bar there was even an entire row of blue liquor bottles—Bols, Alizé, Bombay Sapphire, Pinnacle, Hpnotiq, Blue Ice.

Pike and Tone were sitting at a table close to the bar. The tabletop was covered in empty glasses.

"One day," Pike said as he stared at the bar, "I'm going to start at one end of that row of blue bottles and keep going till I reach the other end." He was speaking too slowly, and some of his words were slurred.

"I thought you'd already done that," Tone said. He had drunk just as much as Pike but didn't show it.

"Nah. I've just picked a few here and there. I'm not as organized as you are, my friend."

"Planning," Tone agreed. "It's the answer to everything." He looked around as if seeing the bar for the first time. "Why is this place so blue?"

"Now that's something I do know," Pike said. "I asked the barman once. He said it's because blue's a cold color. It makes people feel uncomfortable, so they drink more and they drink faster. Good for business."

"What if they don't come at all because it's cold and uncomfortable?"

"It's right by the university, man. And it's the cheapest bar this side of town. Who's not going to come?"

"Brain Stew" faded out and Pike took the opportunity to jump onto his chair.

"Pay attention, you slobs! I've got an important announcement to make. We have in our midst a great man." He waved an arm at Tone and almost fell off his chair. The bar erupted in applause, mostly at Pike's near disaster. "My buddy here, Tone Zhang, is a fucking genius at physics. He's just been awarded Kevin's prize for...some shit to do with freezing stuff."

"Hey, Pike," someone shouted. "You're in the physics department. How come you didn't win a prize?"

Everyone, including Pike, laughed. "I...I could win. I choose not to. I'm just a regular guy. I don't want all the attention." He burped loudly and swayed dangerously on his chair.

"Anyway, we're not here to celebrate me." He raised his glass high. "To Tone. A fucking genius and my friend."

Pike downed his drink in one. Everyone cheered and downed theirs.

"Shooters for everyone," Pike yelled. "Something blue."

The cheering redoubled. Pike half climbed, half fell back down into his seat and grinned stupidly at Tone.

"You're an idiot," Tone said, returning the grin. "But thank you. I appreciated that. It's not Kevin's prize though—it's the Kelvin Fellowship."

"Whatever. This crowd wouldn't know Kelvin from his ass."

The server placed a couple of blue shooters on the table.

Tone stared at his drink thoughtfully. "You know, Pike," he said, "I envy you."

Pike laughed. "You envy *me*? You? The golden boy? You've got everything, Tone—brains, recognition, a ticket out of this shitty place and a beautiful girl. Are you trying to tell me you envy a lazy, sad, overweight loser just because he has a cool car and money?"

"No," Tone said, "although the car's nice." Pike laughed and Tone smiled. "I envy how easy life is for you. You take things as they come, and you get along with everyone. Nothing seems to bother you. I wake up during the night worrying that something's going to go horribly wrong, that I won't be able to achieve all the things I want to. I don't know what I would do if something really important to me went off the rails and there was nothing I could do about it."

"Don't worry, Tone—you're set. Nothing's going to go wrong. You're going to MIT to become the world authority on whatever the hell it is that you do. You'll end up with the Nobel Prize." Pike smiled ruefully, downed his shooter and waved for another round. "Me though? Yeah, I can get on with the Harrys of this world and party with the best of them, but I'm the one living on the edge. You know that the car, the money, the good life—they could vanish in a minute. And they will if I flunk a year. My dad will cut me off in an instant."

"I find it hard to believe he wouldn't give you a second chance."

"Are you kidding? You don't know my dad. He's slaved all his life, making a shitload of money, for one reason and one reason only—so I get the education he never had. And that has to be a degree in something he respects, like engineering or mathematics."

"Or physics."

Pike nodded. "Pretty much anything I have no interest in."

The server arrived with two more drinks. She noticed that Tone hadn't touched his last and placed both in front of Pike. Neither of them complained.

"What *are* you interested in?" Tone asked.

"Not physics, that's for sure," Pike said. He stared morosely at the empty glasses in front of him.

"Your dad puts the pressure on you. My pressure comes from in here." Tone tapped his forehead. "But it's from my dad just the same."

Pike looked up. "How so?"

"My dad had nothing. He worked in a factory, breathing in chemicals he didn't even know the names of. His only hope was to live long enough to see his kids get the same crap jobs he had. I was eleven when he died, and I swore I would kill myself before I lived his life. I slaved over books, passed exams, won scholarships, went to university and came over here—all to escape my dad's world. You know, sometimes when I wake up in the night in a sweat, it's because I've just had a dream that the next morning I'll be getting on a plane to go back to a job in my dad's factory."

"So I guess we're not too different," Pike said. "We made different choices, but for the same reasons."

"Maybe," Tone acknowledged. "It sucks that there are always at least two possible choices, but you're only allowed one decision."

"Yeah," Pike said, lifting one of his shooters. "I can choose to drink this or not." He downed it in one go and slammed the empty glass back on the table. "Decision made."

Tone laughed bitterly and stared at the untouched shooter in front of him. "You think I've got it all, Pike—that I'm confident and in charge of my life—but it's all bullshit. When I was a kid, I lived in terror of screwing up, of saying something stupid in front of my classmates. If a girl talked to me, I either froze and said nothing or blurted out something really dumb. Everyone would laugh at me, and I would lie awake all night wishing I were dead. One night I even sat on the rail of a bridge, wondering what it would be like to just slip off into the water below."

"But you didn't," Pike said, struggling to find something positive to say as he watched his friend sink deeper into misery.

"No. I didn't even have the courage to do that." He looked at Pike and gave him a wry smile. "Point is, that inept, terrified little kid is still here." Tone thumped his chest hard. "I've learned to dress him up in masks. There's one for Tone the physics genius, one for Tone the teaching assistant, even one for Tone the well-dressed guy who can talk to women. But the little bastard's still in there. He's buried deep, but sometimes, like this morning, he peers out around the pile of masks and scares the shit out of me. The masks are me, and I have to believe that they defend me against that little boy. Honestly, Pike, if those masks were torn away, I don't know what I'd do."

Pike stared at Tone, then reached across the table. The two friends clasped hands and squeezed until it hurt.

"Shit, man. This is getting way too heavy. We're here to have fun." He let go of Tone's hand and downed his other shooter. "Hey, where's Theresa? She should be here. Did you call her and tell her where we are? I thought you guys were going out for dinner."

"Forget Theresa." Tone waved dismissively. "This morning was important, and she didn't come."

"This morning was important for her too," Pike pointed out.

"With that little shit Quigley?" Tone said bitterly.

"Well, he might be an asshole, but he's got influence in the world Theresa wants to get into. She thinks he might be giving her a big role that will get her noticed."

"That's not all he'd like to give her."

"Jesus, Tone. Theresa would never cheat on you with Quigley. Just give her a call."

He shook his head. "She had her chance." He stood up. "I'm done here. Let's go."

"Sure. Just let me settle up." Pike went to the bar and paid his bill, which was substantial. The two then wove their way between the tables and out into the cool night air.

"Thanks," Tone said as they set off on their erratic course home. "We going to the range tomorrow?"

"I promised you, didn't I? We'll go and break in that new toy of yours. Blow away a few targets."

"Where's the gun now?"

"I put it in the drawer beside your bed. I didn't want to carry it around in my backpack forever. I've already been scared shitless once because of that."

Tone's brow furrowed. "When? What happened?"

"Didn't I tell you? I was coming back from Harry's this morning with the Ruger in the backpack, and I got pulled over." Pike recounted the story, including every detail. "I damn near threw up," he concluded. "But you know what?"

"What?"

"The cop had seen me reaching into the backseat and just wanted to warn me that it was a dangerous thing to do, that I might have an accident."

Tone started to laugh, and Pike joined in. Soon they were laughing hysterically, holding on to each other to keep from falling over.

"Thoughtful of him," Tone said when they had calmed down a bit. And, arm in arm, the two friends continued down the darkened street.

When Tone woke up his head ached, his mouth felt as if it were stuffed with cotton wool, and he needed to pee. He kept his eyes closed as the previous evening came back to him—drinking with Pike, stories about Harry and cops. Tone hadn't drunk that much since his freshman year. He hated the loss of control. On the other hand, he had to admit it had been fun at the Blue Bar. If only Theresa had been there. He reached an arm over to find the other side of the bed empty. She hadn't been at home when he and Pike staggered in sometime after midnight. She still wasn't home now.

Tone sat up slowly, fighting the pounding in his head. He hoped his head felt better before Pike took him to the shooting range. The revolver! Pike said he had put it somewhere...oh yes, the drawer by the bed.

Gingerly Tone rolled to the side. He pulled the drawer open and there it was, gleaming silver with a black handgrip, nestled beside a brown box announcing *Personal Defense .357 Magnum, 158 grain. Hydra-Shok.* Whatever that meant.

Tone lifted the revolver out of the drawer and slid the red ribbon off the barrel. The gun was small but felt reassuringly heavy and solid. He'd never handled a revolver, so he resisted the temptation to try to open the chamber.

Instead he aimed at items in the room, pretend shooting his shoe in the corner and the ceiling light. He was taking aim at the door handle when it turned, the door swung open and Theresa appeared.

"Oh my god, Tone! What are you doing?"

"Nothing," he said. He hurriedly dropped the gun back in the drawer and pushed it shut. "It's a present from Pike. Don't worry—there's no ammunition in it. We're going out to the range later. Do you want to come?"

"No way. You know I hate guns." She stepped into the room and stared at Tone slumped on their bed. "You're beginning to scare me."

He decided to go on the offensive. "You didn't come home last night. Where were you?" As he asked, a knot of fear formed in his unsettled stomach. What if Theresa had spent the night with Quigley? What if she said it was all over between them?

"We were working on the play. It got late, so I just stayed in my residence room."

Tone sighed with relief, even though a tiny part of his mind questioned whether Theresa would tell him if she was sleeping with Quigley.

"You didn't come to the Blue Bar."

"Like I said, we got wrapped up in the play. Allen gave me a copy of the script, and I was reading through it." Theresa dug into her shoulder bag and pulled out a thick wad of pages, waving them at Tone as if to prove what she'd said. "Time got away from me. Anyway, you didn't call."

"I told you yesterday morning that we were going there. *You* could have called. It was important to me." He silently cursed the whine in his voice.

Theresa's face relaxed. "I'm sorry. I'll make it up to you." She moved into the room and sat on the end of the bed. "You look like crap," she said with a smile.

Tone couldn't help but return the smile. "Pike and I tied one on last night."

"That's not like you."

"I was lonely. I missed you. And the meeting in the morning went badly."

"Was Seeger a pompous ass as usual?"

"Of course, and you know how I hate impromptu speeches. That's why I wanted you there. I was nervous."

Theresa placed the script on the bedside table, moved up beside Tone and stroked his cheek. "I'm sorry," she said. "Was it really bad?"

"I managed to insult Seeger, the physics department and the entire university."

"I always knew you were accomplished," she said, laughing. "Don't worry. You don't need them. We'll soon be at MIT, and everything will be wonderful." She nodded at the script on the table. "I think my meeting yesterday went a bit better than yours. Allen's written a play. Actually, he's written the third act of a play that was never completed. To celebrate the anniversaries of the playwright's birth and death. And"—she smiled and leaned even closer to Tone—"he's offered me one of the lead roles." She stood up and did a pirouette in the middle of the floor. "It's a big deal," she said as she danced around the room. "Everyone in the theater community will be there. If I do a good job—no, if I do a *great* job—I'll be noticed by important people. There's no telling where it might lead. I'm so excited!"

Theresa did a final pirouette and flung herself down beside Tone, who managed to suppress a groan as his aching head bounced against the headboard and his bladder threatened to explode. He loved Theresa's enthusiasm but hated that he couldn't share it. He'd never be able to see the point in making up stories on the stage, and there were practical things to consider.

"When's this production going to be put on?"

She snuggled next to him. "Allen didn't say exactly. Next month, I think. Probably close to the end. I hope so. There's a lot of work to be done. Speaking of which, I'm going to be spending more time in residence. It's right by the theater, so it's really convenient if we're working late. You can come too. I know the bed's small, but it'll be cozy. Starting today, we're going to be rehearsing nonstop. It'll be insane, but it's so"—she paused, searching for the right word—"intoxicating."

"I'll need to go to MIT at the end of the month."

"We'll work it out." Nothing could stand in the way of Theresa's enthusiasm. "If you have to go first, I can follow."

"Is the theater this important to you?"

"It's as important to me as physics is to you."

Tone said nothing.

Theresa added, "And it might be as important to you as well."

"What do you mean?"

"I wasn't going to tell you now, but I guess this is as good a time as any. Allen wants you to be in the play as well."

"He wants *what*?" Tone couldn't believe what he was hearing.

"He wants you to be in the play too. There are three main characters. Allen will play the playwright himself—Neil Peterson. I'll play Lily, the female lead. And you'll play Hill Chao."

Tone laughed. "This is insane. I can't act."

"That's what Allen wants—someone who can bring a fresh perspective to the work."

"Someone who will make fool of himself and be laughed at, more like."

"Acting's not like the spontaneous speeches you hate making. You control everything beforehand. In fact, it's the ultimate exercise in control. You're not only controlling another character's life, but you're also manipulating how the audience reacts to that character. Done right, you can make people feel whatever you want—happy, sad, scared. It's immensely powerful." She could see she wasn't convincing him. "Take time to think about it. You don't have to say yes or no right away."

"Yes, I do, and the answer's no. I'm not going to be in Allen Quigley's play, and I don't think you should be either."

Anger swept over him. Her affectionate cuddling, he realized, was just to persuade him to take on a ridiculous role in Quigley's stupid play.

Theresa looked so hurt that Tone almost apologized. But his anger was too strong. "And I'm not going to move into your tiny room in residence. Isn't it enough that we're going to California?"

For a moment Tone thought she was going to burst into tears, but her face hardened.

"No, California's *not* enough," she said, her voice cold. "It's not as if you applied for the MIT fellowship because it included six months in California. Don't try to take credit for that." She jumped off the bed, grabbed a gym bag from the closet and began stuffing clothes into it. "I'm doing Allen's play. You can do whatever the hell you want."

Tone watched in horror as his life fell apart. He wanted to do something, but he didn't know what. His head was throbbing like a bass drum, and he was terrified he was about to pee the bed.

"Theresa..." he said weakly.

She finished packing, zipped up her bag and opened the door. Then she stopped and turned around.

"I'm sorry we fought," she said. "I really hoped you would be open to this, and that the play would be something we could share, but apparently not. If you change your mind, you know where the theater is. We'll be there all day, every day."

Then she was gone.

"Fuck!" Tone exclaimed. Feeling worse than he had when he first woke up, he struggled out of bed, stumbled to the bathroom and noisily emptied his bladder. He took a long shower, resisted the temptation to return to bed and got dressed. He felt marginally better now—at least physically.

His stomach rumbled as he headed out of the bathroom in search of coffee. Had he even eaten supper the night before? He vaguely remembered a mountain of cheese-drenched nachos. Were the nachos blue?

Tone was surprised to see Pike slouched on the couch, playing his video game with the sound turned off.

"Have you been there all night?"

"Pretty much," he said, not taking his eyes off the screen. "I slept for a few hours. Your fight with Theresa woke me up."

"We weren't having a fight."

"Okay. Whatever. Man, you were wasted last night." Pike turned toward him. "And you don't look that great this morning. There's coffee made."

"Thanks," Tone said as he headed for the kitchen. "I need food. You want some?"

"Sure." Pike turned back to his game.

The sound of drawers opening and closing and cupboard doors banging reached Pike. "Why doesn't that woman put things back where they're supposed to go?" he heard Tone say.

Pike ignored the question. But he couldn't ignore the loud sound of breaking glass and the yell that came next. "You okay?" he called.

"No," Tone shouted back. "I'm not okay! Why do you have to put your beer at the front of the shelf in the fridge?"

Pike decided it would be better not to answer that question. He went on playing and half listening to Tone cleaning up and thumping pans onto the stove. After a while he chanced a "How's it going in there?"

"Fine. The bacon and eggs are almost done. You want toast?"

"Sure."

The sound of the smoke alarm going off shattered what little tranquility was left.

"You sure you're fine?" Pike called, pausing his game.

"Fuck off!"

Pike sighed and hauled himself off the sofa. He stood on a dining-room chair and pressed the Cancel button on the alarm. Tone came in from the kitchen carrying two plates and placed them on the table.

"Breakfast is served," he said.

Pike sat down and stared at the plate before him. He picked up a blackened rasher of bacon and dropped it on the edge of his plate. It made a far louder noise than bacon should. "Whoa."

"Sorry," Tone said. "But it's better than nothing."

"I'm not sure about that." Pike got up, went to the kitchen and brought back a bottle of ketchup. He squirted a thick layer over his bacon and eggs and began crunching his way through his breakfast.

Tone smiled for the first time that morning. "I feel like shit. And you're right—Theresa and I did have a fight. She's got a lead role in some new play by that little prick Quigley. She thinks it's a big deal that will lead to big things."

"That's great," Pike said. "She's got talent, Tone. She deserves a chance."

"It's just playacting." Tone dipped his toast in an egg and chewed morosely. "She's going to be incredibly busy just when I'm getting ready to make the move to MIT."

Pike thought it worked the other way as well—that Tone would be so wrapped up in his move, he wouldn't be able to give support to Theresa—but he said nothing.

"She's going to stay in residence all the time now," Tone continued. "She wants to be close to the theater and on her own—at least, I hope she wants to be on her own."

"What do you mean by *that*?"

Tone shrugged. "Nothing." He pushed his virtually untouched plate away.

"Okay," Pike said through the last mouthful of ketchup-soaked toast. He sat back. "You ready for some serious gunplay at the range?"

"Hell, yeah," Tone said enthusiastically. "Let's do it."

CHAPTER SEVEN

Nanjing, Jiangsu

Morning, December 14, 1937

Still gasping for breath, Lily struggles to her feet and scrambles after Hill. Other women are following the bound prisoners, begging for their husbands, brothers or sons to be released. Japanese soldiers are forcing them back with their rifles.

Hill looks back over his shoulder as he's dragged forward. The pleading look on his face stops Lily in her tracks. She can't save him—not this way. With what she hopes is an encouraging wave, she turns away from Hill. As the first snowflakes swirl down around her, she forces her way through the crowd and into the more open streets.

As Lily runs frantically toward the Japanese embassy, she prays for two things: that the Japanese don't kill their prisoners immediately after they get them out of the Safety Zone, and that Shimada is at the embassy. If he's not there or if she can't find him, her attempt will be hopeless.

Ignoring the growing pain in her lungs, she forces herself on through the ruined streets.

Approaching the embassy, Lily slows down to get her breathing under control. A Chinese person running toward the Japanese embassy stands a good chance of being shot on sight. When she has calmed down, she approaches the guard by the front gate. She speaks very few Japanese words, so she mimics talking and repeats Shimada's name. The guard stares at her blankly.

"Shimada. Akira Shimada. Please. Please. I must talk to Akira Shimada."

The soldier continues to stare.

Lily imagines Hill's bloody body in a ditch. Then she sees two figures strolling across the embassy courtyard. A short, plump man with thick glasses and a shapeless suit that seems too large for him is deep in conversation with a neatly dressed Japanese soldier. She bursts past the surprised guard and grabs the icy iron railings of the gate.

"Mr. Shimada!" she screams. "Mr. Shimada, they've taken Hill!"

Shimada turns from his conversation and peers at the gate.

"I'm Lily Chan, Hill's friend from the drama department at the university," she shouts frantically. "Do you remember me? Hill's been taken. I think he's going to be killed. You must do something!"

Having recovered from his surprise, the guard grabs Lily by the shoulders and pulls her away from the gate. But she's caught Shimada's attention. The short man is coming toward them. He says something to the guard, who releases his grip on Lily.

"My dear Lily," Shimada says with a smile. "Of course I remember someone as beautiful as you. Now tell me what happened."

Breathlessly Lily recounts the events in the square in front of the church. "I think the prisoners were taken away to be shot," she concludes. "You know that Hill's not a soldier. We must do something quickly."

Shimada thinks for a moment. "And what makes you believe the prisoners were going to be shot?"

Lily doesn't know how to reply. All she has to go on are those bursts of machine-gun fire she heard at the river and a gut feeling that the prisoners in the square were being taken away for execution. She's rescued by the Japanese soldier, who comes up behind Shimada, leans forward and whispers in his ear. They step away and begin an increasingly heated conversation. Lily doesn't understand a word, but it's obvious that Shimada is struggling to convince the soldier of something.

The soldier stares over at Lily. He's wearing a soft cap, a three-quarter-length khaki coat and black leather riding boots. A pistol and a long sword hang from his belt, and the red-and-gold shoulder patches with three silver stars mark him as an officer. Eventually he looks at Shimada and nods. Shimada turns back to the gate, his smile replaced by a worried expression.

"Colonel Masao informs me that there has been an... unfortunate error. Please wait here."

Shimada and the officer disappear around the side of the building, leaving Lily to pace nervously outside the gate. The snow is not getting any heavier, but a thin dusting has begun to coat the ground. She hears distant machine-gun fire. Is Hill dead now? Is she too late? Was she right in coming here instead of following the prisoners? Maybe she could have persuaded them to let Hill go.

She's almost convinced herself to flee back to the square to try to find out where the prisoners have been taken when a black open-topped car turns the corner and stops beside her. Rising Sun flags flap from the front wings. A Japanese soldier is driving, and Masao sits in the front seat, stony-faced. Shimada is in the back and leans over to open the door for her.

"Come and sit by me," he says.

Lily climbs in, and the car moves off along the cleared lane through the rubble from bombed-out buildings.

"Where are we going?" Lily asks as she realizes they're heading away from the church square and out of the Safety Zone.

"You'll see," Shimada says mysteriously.

Masao barks something over his shoulder.

"Colonel Masao is doing us a great favor," Shimada tells Lily. "In return, you must agree to forget anything that you see."

Lily agrees without understanding what she's agreeing to.

As they travel through Nanjing, Lily is overwhelmed by what she sees. The snow clouds seem thicker and lower now, smothering the stricken city. Although it's still morning, it's almost dark enough to be twilight. The light is flat, and all the color is drained from the scene. Nanjing is a world reduced to shades of gray.

Every building they pass is damaged—some are nothing more than piles of blackened rubble—and dark smoke still rises from smoldering fires in many places. Unlike the Safety Zone, where any open space is crowded with refugees, this part of the city is deserted except for the bodies that lie everywhere, many of them women and children. Lily is revolted to see skinny dogs feeding on some of them. On one ruined wall, a row of human heads stare at her with dead eyes. The air is heavy with dust, smoke and snow. It has the harsh smell of fire and, underneath, the sickly sweet smell of death and decay.

Shimada offers Lily a handkerchief to hold over her nose, but she keeps looking. The scenes of horror are hard to face, but she forces herself to take everything in. Despite her promise to Shimada, she intends to remember—to bear witness.

At last the car nears the river and pulls up at the edge of a wide-open area. Lily stands up in the back of the car and gasps.

"Is this where Hill was taken?"

"Colonel Masao says this is where all the captured enemy soldiers are taken," Shimada explains.

Lily scans the area in front of the car. The snow is falling more thickly now, and she can just see the heads and shoulders of figures standing in the large fenced enclosure that occupies most of the open ground. They're are all men, some of whom still wear the tattered remnants of uniforms. But the remarkable thing is the silence. Not one person in the thousands in the compound is talking with his neighbor or pleading with the guards. All stand immobile and stare sullenly forward. No one even turns his head when the car pulls up.

As Lily surveys the scene, a part of her is daunted by the size of the task facing her, but another part is hopeful. If this many people are here, Hill must be among them somewhere.

"They can't all be soldiers," she says as she peers through the snow. "Most of them are in civilian clothes, and some are boys who can't be more than ten or twelve years old."

Shimada and Masao have a short conversation.

"The colonel assures me," Shimada explains curtly, "that everyone in there has been either captured in battle or found with a weapon or a bruised shoulder."

"A bruised shoulder?"

"A sign that they have recently fired a weapon," Shimada says.

"But that's impossible," Lily blurts. "There must two or three thousand people there. Not all of them can have bruised shoulders. And some of those boys are too small to even lift a rifle, let alone fire one."

Masao says something to Shimada, steps out of the car and goes over to talk to an officer who is overseeing a group of bound prisoners being pushed into the enclosure. Lily thinks that what Masao said sounded like an order.

"None of this is your concern," Shimada says. "We have ten minutes to find Hill."

"Ten minutes! He has to give us longer."

"We are lucky to get that. Now I suggest that instead of arguing about how long we have, we split up to cover more ground. If we go around the enclosure in opposite directions, we have a good chance of finding him."

Without waiting for an answer, Shimada leaves the car and walks toward the enclosure. When he gets there he begins moving along the fence, scanning the crowd.

Lily looks in the opposite direction. The land slopes up to a ridge; on the other side must be the river. As she climbs out of the car she notices several soldiers opening a section of the fence and hustling a large group of bound prisoners out. One of them looks familiar.

"Hill!" she yells, a surge of joy rushing through her. She runs up the slope toward the group. "Hill, we've come to get you."

He turns, searching for the source of the voice. He sees Lily running toward him and steps away from the group. The rope prevents him from going far, and a guard moves over and casually hits him on the side of the head with his rifle butt. Hill collapses like an empty sack. The soldier kicks him and shouts something at the other prisoners, who keep moving, dragging Hill along the ground.

Lily reaches the Japanese soldier, yelling for all she's worth. "We've come to get this man. His arrest was a mistake. He's not a soldier. Shimada and Colonel Masao are here."

She points down the slope to Shimada and Masao, who, alerted by her cries, are heading their way.

The soldier understands nothing that is being said to him, and he's confused at being shouted at by a Chinese girl. Nevertheless, he follows Lily's arm and sees a senior officer and a civilian coming toward him. Lily pushes past him to Hill, who is groggily getting to his feet. From the corner of her eye she sees over the ridge to the rocky shore of the wide, sluggishly moving river.

"You're safe now," she says, embracing Hill. "Shimada's here." She pulls back and unties the coarse rope around his arms. "We'll take you back to the university."

When she gets no response from Hill, she raises her eyes to look into his face. A trickle of blood is running down from his temple. Instead of looking at her with a smile or an expression of relief, he's staring in horror over her shoulder.

"What?" she asks, turning to look at the river. Gradually it dawns on her that what she glimpsed before is not a rocky shore. The "rocks" are a tangle of thousands of human bodies.

Confused, Lily takes a couple of steps to the top of the ridge. "Oh God," she gasps as the full scale of the frightful scene unveils itself.

As far as she can see in either direction, the entire shore of the river is a mass of bodies. They extend to where the dark, oily swell of the water covers them. On either side of her, soldiers in sandbagged machine-gun pits turn to stare.

Lily's legs go weak, and she's on the verge of collapsing when Hill catches her. He turns her away from the atrocious sight just as Masao and Shimada arrive.

"We must go. Now!" Shimada orders.

Hill supports Lily as they are hustled back to the car. On the way Masao starts shouting at Shimada, who visibly shrinks under the verbal barrage. When they arrive at the car, Hill, Lily and Shimada climb into the backseat, but Masao spins on his heel and stalks back to the enclosure.

"What did he say to you?" Hill asks as the driver begins reversing the car.

"Colonel Masao says you have seen what you should not have," Shimada explains. "He wants to arrest you."

"He can't do that!" Hill blurts out. "We haven't done anything wrong."

"He is a Japanese army officer, and you are Chinese. He can do whatever he likes," Shimada says. "You are both incredibly lucky. You must go back to the university and never leave the Safety Zone again."

The three sit in silence as the car heads away through the snow.

"There is one more thing," Shimada adds. "I should not be telling you this, but Colonel Masao is planning to carry out a sweep of the university."

"What for?" Hill asks.

"To look for hidden soldiers. I am sure he will find none. I think he is only doing it to make life difficult for you. He does not think the Safety Zone is a good idea, but he cannot do anything about it. He will do whatever he can to find an excuse to close the zone down. You must all be extremely careful."

"When is he planning this sweep?" Hill asks.

"He did not say, but soon. It could even be this afternoon."

Hill puts his arm around Lily and holds her tight. She's weeping quietly. A shudder passes through both of them as a burst of machine-gun fire echoes from the riverbank.

CHAPTER EIGHT

Ashford, Ohio

Present Day

Pike pulled off the country road into a gravel parking lot in front of a log building with heavily barred windows. A faded sign above the door read *Gentlemen's Sport and Game Club*.

"Fancy name for a cabin in the woods," Tone commented.

"Some English guy thought he could create a country club here," Pike explained as he exited the car. They each grabbed a backpack from the trunk and headed for the door. "He introduced trout into a local pond, imported a shitload of pheasants and built a clay-pigeon shooting range out back and a classy bar in front. Then he sat down and waited for all the gentry in tweed jackets to show up. A few locals came and fished his pond out in a couple of years. All the pheasants died the first real cold winter we had. And no one could see the point of shooting clay plates flying through the air when there were deer running around in the woods. On top of that, the fancy whiskey he sold was twice the price of anything in the local bars, so the English guy went bankrupt pretty quickly. He sold the place for a song about ten years ago and went home. Morrison's been running it as a regular gun shop and shooting range ever since."

"Doesn't look like he's getting rich either."

"He gets by." Pike stopped outside the door. "Mostly because he does occasional odd jobs that don't require any paperwork or a declaration on an IRS return. I suspect he's the source of your gun, but it's best not to say anything about it, okay?"

"Fine by me. I just want to shoot the thing."

Pike pushed the door open and ushered Tone inside. A large rough stone fireplace dominated one wall of the room. There was a sad moth-eaten elk's head mounted above it. Opposite was an oak bar that wouldn't have looked out of place in a spaghetti western, except that there were racks of guns where the bottles should have been. A middle-aged black man in a stained baseball cap stood behind the bar, his eyes closed as he sang along to a hip-hop song blasting out of two speakers set at either end of the bar. He wasn't someone Tone would consider messing with. He obviously worked out, and the cold look he gave the two when they walked in sent a chill down Tone's spine.

"You Harry's boys?" the man asked.

"Yeah, Morrison," Pike said. "I've been here a couple of times with Harry."

Morrison nodded. "You I've seen before. Who's this guy?"

"Just a friend who wants to shoot a few rounds in peace," Pike said.

"Indoor or outdoor?"

"Indoor."

"Forty bucks," Morrison said, holding out a hand.

Pike peeled two twenties off a roll and handed them over.

Morrison's hand remained stretched out. "As I recall, Harry owes me twenty."

Pike peeled off another bill and passed it over. "Harry's not doing so well. He's laying low right now."

Morrison nodded again and led them through a back door. Six booths faced long alleys. Regular round targets hung at the end of three alleys. Human silhouettes were the targets for the other three.

"Targets or people?" Morrison asked.

Pike glanced at Tone, who looked distinctly uncomfortable. "Targets?"

Tone nodded.

Morrison pointed to the second booth. "Don't shoot yourselves," he said and left.

Tone dug the revolver out of his backpack and laid it down on the table in the booth. He placed the box of ammunition beside it.

Pike reached into his backpack and pulled out a can of Budweiser. He popped the top and took a swig. "Okay, a couple of things you need to know. First, this is no toy." He stepped forward into the booth, put down his beer and opened the ammunition box. He took out a snub-nosed bullet. "One of these will make a real mess of your insides, so be careful. Never assume that your gun is unloaded. Always check. Always be thinking of the gun—where it's pointing and what would happen if it went off."

Tone nodded. Pike put the bullet down and picked up the revolver.

"This isn't like the cowboy guns in the movies. It's dual-action. That means you don't have to cock the hammer between shots. It will keep firing every time you pull the trigger. It holds five shells in the chamber." When he flipped a button, the round magazine slid out, revealing five holes. He began loading.

Tone listened as Pike went over the features and showed him the safety catch, but his eyes kept drifting to the target hanging at the other end of the shooting alley.

At last Pike finished his explanation. He unloaded the gun, retrieved his beer and watched as Tone loaded it.

"Go for it," he said, stepping back.

Tone felt unreasonably excited. He was only going to fire a few shots at a round paper target in a firing range, but he felt powerful. The cold metal weapon in his hand seemed the very epitome of control.

Tone spread his legs and held the revolver with both hands, just as he'd seen it done on TV. The kick surprised him, and the sound in the enclosed space left his ears ringing, but neither dampened the thrill he felt. He aimed and fired again, and again, and again, and again.

When the hammer clicked on an empty chamber, Pike came around the partition and pushed the button to bring the target swinging toward them. He unclipped it and held it up to the light streaming through the window behind them. There were only two bright spots where the light shone through. Neither was close to the bull's-eye.

"I only hit it twice?" Tone said, his disappointment obvious.

"You imagined a nice tight cluster around the bull's-eye?" Pike asked with a smile as he took another swig of beer.

"No," Tone admitted, "but better than this."

"It's not as easy as it looks. Okay, reload."

Remembering Pike's instructions, Tone reloaded. Pike led him through a few more magazines, showing him how to hold the gun, aim precisely and take account of the kick.

By the time they'd used half of the ammunition Tone was managing to get five shots on the target, but only the occasional one was anywhere close to the bull's-eye. His excitement was waning.

"There must be something wrong with the sights," he complained.

Pike reloaded the gun, pushed Tone behind him and fired five rapid shots at a fresh target. When he wound the target in, Tone was impressed to see five holes in a loose cluster around the bull's-eye.

"I think the sights are okay," he said. "But then, I've always looked at things a bit differently." Pike dropped his empty beer can into the garbage. "That's probably enough for today. We want to save some bullets for next time."

Pike watched as Tone tucked the gun and the remaining ammunition into his backpack. He saw the disappointment on Tone's face. "Don't worry, man," he said. "It takes practice."

They walked back through the shop, thanking Morrison as they went. In the parking lot Pike produced two more beers from his pack and handed one to Tone. They leaned against a split-rail fence and took long drinks.

"That tastes good," Tone said.

"Hair of the dog, as they say."

They drank in silence for a while before Pike ventured a comment. "I'm sorry you and Theresa fought this morning, but things are going pretty good for you both. You've got your plan. Always the man with a plan," he added with a laugh. "You and Theresa are going to MIT. That's great. She thinks it's great too, and she's kind of important to the plan, right?"

Tone nodded but didn't say anything.

"I think she wants what you want, but this play is important to her. When you run down theater, saying it's just play-acting, it hurts her, and she lashes out. Can't you just give her some support in this? When the play's over, you'll head off to MIT and live happily ever after."

"I wish it were that simple."

"It could be, if you give Theresa a bit of space to do what she wants."

A bit of space to run off with Quigley, Tone thought. But he didn't say that. Instead he said, "Quigley wants me to be in the play."

"You!" Pike almost choked on his beer. "He's dumber than I thought. How can he think anyone would want to see you onstage?"

Tone laughed. "I agree. I'm not an actor, but Theresa said that's what Quigley wants. Anyway, I said no."

Pike sipped his beer thoughtfully. "Maybe you should think about it a bit more."

"You're kidding me, right?"

"No." He shook his head. "Think about it, man. You've gotten what's most important to you—the MIT thing. If you don't seriously mess up, Theresa's going to be a part of that. Now she's gotten what's important to her, so why don't you be a part of it?"

"You think?"

"Look, I'm not a sophisticated ladies' man like you. I'm a slob just trying to get by, and I know it. But I also know Theresa's worth fighting for, and if that involves standing onstage for an hour or two, what the hell!"

Tone drained his beer. "I'll think about it."

"Hey, that's all I'm saying. Now, you ready to head over to the campus? I'm up for a burger for lunch."

"I'm not sure my stomach's up for a burger yet, and I don't want to be wandering around with a gun in my backpack. Just drop me off at the house."

"Probably a good plan," Pike agreed.

The two friends dumped their empties, climbed into the car and headed onto the highway in a spray of gravel.

Pike burped loudly as he exited the cafeteria. Beer, fries and a burger with all the trimmings—was there a better lunch in the world? At least there was something in America he enjoyed. He strolled across campus, debating whether to go to class or to head back to the house for a nap. Then he spotted Theresa heading toward the theater. "Hey!" he shouted.

Theresa stopped and waited for him to join her. "This isn't a question I usually ask when I see someone walking across a university campus, but what are you doing here?" she asked.

"You're so funny you should be on the stage—oh, wait."

Theresa laughed, and Pike grinned. "Been in for a burger," he said. "Tone made breakfast this morning—a burnt offering of bacon, eggs and toast. It took almost a full bottle of ketchup to make it edible. I needed some good food."

"You can put flour on the bacon to keep it from burning, or wrap it in paper towels and cook it in the microwave."

"I think I love you."

Theresa laughed, but Pike suddenly looked serious. "What *am* I doing here?" he said thoughtfully. "I actually think about that a lot. I never wanted to come here—to America, yes, but not to Ashford or Eastern University, and certainly not to the physics department. I know nothing about physics and have no desire to learn more. And then I don't say anything in the few classes I go to because I'm terrified of looking stupid. My life has become all about maximum avoidance and minimum work. I'm only still here because of Tone—he helps me out with my assignments. Well, you know that." Pike kicked at a small rock on the path. "So why *am* I here?"

"Your dad?"

"Yeah. I'm living the life my dad wanted to live. I'm here, barely surviving this really shitty existence, so he can be a man of status back home, boasting about his brilliant son studying physics in America." Pike laughed bitterly. "I don't mind the America bit—nice cars, good movies, plenty of bars. And I could study Asian history here as well as anywhere. But my dad would have a fit if I did that. He thinks studying the past's a waste of time. Only the future matters to him. So I'm trapped. If I give up and go home, I'm a failure. But to be happy, I have to break my dad's heart. Sucks, eh? Every time I see some Chinese dropout head home in disgrace, I think it could be me—and I envy him. I'm so close to the edge."

Pike looked so desolate that Theresa couldn't help giving him a hug. He shrugged her off. "Thanks, Theresa," he said. "I appreciate it, really, but I don't want sympathy. I just want to be free to make my own choices."

They stopped walking and stood under a large maple tree.

"I don't think you're alone," Theresa said. "A lot of Chinese students feel the same kind of pressure you do. Tone feels it too, just in a different way."

"He puts the pressure on himself. That means he can choose to remove the pressure—to let it go."

"I'm not sure he can. He's been really wound up lately. I'm glad he got this fellowship. I'd hate to think what would have happened if it hadn't come through. It would have killed him."

"You *are* going with him to MIT, right?"

She hesitated too long.

"Jesus, Theresa! If you don't go it'll tear him apart."

"I'm not sure it would, Pike. I'm not as important to Tone as MIT is."

Pike opened his mouth to argue, but she didn't give him a chance. "I didn't sleep much last night, but I did a lot of thinking. Allen's play is all about choices—even difficult and dangerous ones in the middle of war. I began to wonder, Am I making my own choices? Yesterday I assumed I would go to MIT with Tone, that this role in Allen's play would get me noticed and I could build on that in California. Today I'm not so sure.

"There's nothing at MIT for me. California would be nice, but...I want what I do onstage to be important, and there are better places to achieve that than California. Even in China—the place I ran away from—theater is a more important medium than it is here. I honestly don't know what I'll do. I need to think more. But whatever I do, it'll be *my* decision. I won't be forced into making choices I don't want to make."

Theresa stared across the courtyard at the front of the theater. "That's sort of what Allen's play is about. Peterson—the guy the theater's named after—he went to China in 1937 because he was interested in Chinese theater and opera. He went to Nanjing, where he fell in love with Lily, the leader of the student drama group there. That's who I play," she said with a smile. "The beautiful Lily."

"Great casting," said Pike, returning the smile.

"Peterson, Lily and a Chinese student called Hill—who I think was also in love with Lily—got caught up in the Japanese attack on the city and the massacres and rapes that followed. When it was all over, Peterson came back to America and became a brilliant playwright, but there was one play he could never finish. Allen's play is about what happened to those three in Nanjing in 1937. Peterson and the others made choices during the horror of those days. We have no idea what those choices were or what pressures were on each of them. But whatever happened in Nanjing, Peterson was never able to come to terms with it.

"That's what we're exploring in Allen's play—it's his attempt to complete it for Peterson. It's not just a piece of history that happened long ago and doesn't matter today. We all make choices every day, and we have to live with the consequences. There are never second chances. I think that's what Allen wants to bring out, using the mystery of Peterson's unfinished play as a mirror. It's difficult, brave and worthwhile, and I want to help him achieve something exceptional."

"And it won't hurt that Allen's hanging off the coattails of this famous Peterson guy."

"I don't think that's fair, Pike. Allen loves theater, and he's fascinated by the mystery of what Peterson did in China. He's done a lot of research into that time."

Pike looks a bit sheepish. "Oddly enough, so have I."

"Really?"

"Yeah. I know we learned a lot about it in school—the Long March and so on—but it was all way more complicated than we were told. I'm finding lots of old books in the library archives, old diaries and stuff published back in the thirties, forties and fifties. Most of them are written in Chinese, so I doubt anyone here's ever read them. I wonder where they came from."

"Allen told me that Peterson left boxes of his notes and papers to the university in his will. Maybe he collected books to research the play he never finished and left them to the library as well?"

"Could be. Anyway, wherever they're from, I'm having more fun reading them than I've ever had working on a physics problem."

"You've got to get into history, Pike. That's what you love."

"Yeah, well, maybe one day."

"Anyway, thanks for listening, Pike." Theresa gave her friend a hug. "I gotta go. We're doing a read-through, and this was just a short break."

"And I have a nap waiting for me at home."

Theresa laughed and headed for the theater. Pike stood and watched her until she disappeared through the door. With a sigh, he turned toward the parking lot.

Theresa was deep in thought as she entered the drama building. What Pike had said about the pressures of being in

America had raised a question that tied in with what she'd been thinking about the previous night. She knew about Tone's reasons for coming to America, and Pike's, but why had *she* come?

She didn't have an answer when she turned a corner and saw Tone leaning against the wall outside the theater door. He looked nervous and smiled shyly as he pushed off the wall. He held up the copy of the script Theresa had left on the bedside table.

"I read it," he said. "Maybe I'll give it a try."

Theresa rushed forward and threw her arms around him. "I'm so happy you decided to come! You'll be brilliant. Come in and meet everyone."

She led him into the hall. Quigley and several cast members were on the stage in deep conversation. Others were sitting in the seats, reading copies of the script.

"Hi, everyone," Theresa said. "This is Tone. He's going to play Hill."

She quickly ran through everyone's names for Tone, and a chorus of hellos echoed around the hall. Tone responded with a halfhearted wave. Allen jumped off the stage, ran up the aisle and grasped Tone's hand.

"Awesome you could make it. Now we're complete. This is going to be great!" He led them onto the stage and addressed the cast. "Okay, everyone, let's get on with the reading. We'll continue from where we left off before the break." He turned to Tone. "That's Lily speaking at the top of page twenty-six. You come in at the bottom of the page.

This is just a read-through, so don't worry about trying to act. Just read the words. Let's go."

Theresa/Lily: What are we going to do? I'm scared.

Allen/Peterson: That's what I'm asking you. It's you I fear for—you and all the others. This hasn't got anything to do with America. Westerners will be safe, but the Chinese…

Theresa/Lily: It's crowded in here, but I think it's safe. It's the people outside the Safety Zone and those in the countryside I'm frightened for. Doesn't Hill have family in one of the villages nearby?

Allen/Peterson: I don't know. Where is he, anyway? He should be back by now. We need those props.

Theresa/Lily: I worry a lot about Hill. He takes such risks. The streets are filled with Japanese soldiers.

Quigley signaled Tone to take his place beside them. Nervously Tone stepped out from behind the curtain. The stage lights weren't on, so he could see the students sitting in the auditorium and to each side of the stage. He felt as if everyone would be judging him. As he approached, Allen turned to him and said, "Hill! Do you have the props?" Tone swallowed hard. He was sweating too much, but he stumbled through his words.

Tone/Hill: Some. I think enough.

Allen/Peterson: What took you so long?

Tone/Hill: I went to see my family.

Theresa/Lily: That's insanely dangerous. You must persuade them to come into the Safety Zone while there's still time.

Tone/Hill: I'm trying. That's why I went to see them—to persuade my father to bring Mother here. He refuses to leave the house unprotected. I told him that a house, protected or not, is useless when you are dead.

Theresa/Lily: Is he coming in?

Tone/Hill: I don't know.

Tone coughed and lost his place on the page. He shook his head, knowing he was making a dreadful mess of this. Theresa smiled at him and Allen nodded encouragingly. Tone found his place again and went on. As he read his fear faded, and he found that he was focusing more on the words he had to speak. He began to see them as a window into the person who was speaking them. He found himself wondering what Hill would have been thinking and feeling.

Tone/Hill: I'm so worried about them. Japanese soldiers are everywhere, and there are bodies in piles in the streets and all along the riverbank. At any moment they could break into my parents' house and decide they want to steal their pitiful chickens. My father's a proud man. He would try to stop them—and they would kill him. My parents have worked hard all their lives to give me everything I have—an education, a place at the university—and I can't even keep them safe.

Tone stopped and looked around. Gradually he realized that no one else was saying anything. Theresa and Quigley were staring at him.

"Was it that bad?" he asked with a weak smile.

"On the contrary," Quigley said. "It was good. But I didn't write that bit at the end about working hard."

Puzzled, Tone looked down at his script. His lines ended with *they would kill him*. His brow furrowed as he searched the page for the words he was convinced he had seen.

"I'm really sorry," he said. "I guess it just seemed right for Hill to say that. It won't happen again."

"Don't apologize," Quigley said. "It's amazing that you're getting into the character's head so quickly." He turned to address the rest of the cast. "That's probably good for today. Everybody go home and read through your lines. Try to imagine speaking them with the characters you worked with in today's scenes. We'll have another go tomorrow. Let's meet here at three. Thank you all very much. We've made a good beginning. Good work."

The students picked up their packs, shuffled their copies of the script and dispersed through the theater's various exits. Soon only Tone, Allen and Theresa were left.

"You were awesome," Theresa said, giving Tone a hug. "This is going to be so much fun."

"How did you feel your first time behind the footlights?" Allen asked.

"Scared," Tone admitted. "I felt like I was being stared at the whole time. There was no place to hide."

"Stage fright," Theresa said, putting her arm around Tone's shoulder. "It feels like the audience is inside your head—that they know what you're thinking and how terrified you are. It's a special kind of panic."

Allen said jovially, "Don't scare him any more than he is already." He turned to Tone. "It helps when the stage lights are on. You don't really see the audience. It's just dark out there. The only time you see people is when the house lights come up at the end, and you bow to their applause. So it gets better. And anyway, you seemed to relax as you went on."

"I think I did," Tone agreed. "But I still don't know where that extra bit came from."

"Don't worry about it," Allen said. "Go with the character. If you go too far, I'll let you know. For a first-time read-through and with no acting background, you were great. I think you're a natural. All you lack is stage experience. You *are* Hill. It's uncanny, right, Theresa?"

She nodded.

Allen came and stood between them. He put an arm around each of their shoulders. "Now, then, *we few, we happy few, we band of brothers*, I think it's important we spend some time together."

Tone cringed at Quigley's camaraderie and the arm around his shoulder, but Allen didn't seem to notice.

"So I propose that we three stars of this triumph-to-be adjourn posthaste to the nearest hostelry." When Tone looked confused, Allen said, "Let's go for a drink."

Allen jumped off the stage and grabbed his bag and coat from a chair.

Tone brushed his hand over Theresa's arm and whispered, "Will you come home with me tonight? I don't like being on campus if I'm not working. I feel like an outsider."

"I can't," Theresa said. "We're just going for one drink, and then I'm coming back here to do some work on the costumes. I'll probably work late, and then all I'll want is to fall into bed in my room. Tomorrow's going to be even more chaotic than today." She kissed Tone lightly on the cheek. "Well done."

"Come on, you two," Allen said. "Merriment awaits."

Theresa walked to the edge of the stage and jumped down. Tone didn't move.

"I think I'll just head back home," he said. "I drank too much last night, and Pike needs looking after."

"You sure?" Allen asked.

Tone nodded. Theresa gave him a questioning look but followed Allen up the aisle and out the door.

Tone stood for a long time on the stage, staring at the closed door. He wasn't sure why he had refused to go for a drink. He *was* tired after the night before, and the day had been overwhelming—from the thrill of the shooting range to the terror of walking onstage for the first time—but he should have gone. After all, he was doing this to be a part of Theresa's experience. Now she was sharing the experience with Quigley.

He sat down on the edge of the stage. He suddenly felt miserable and very alone.

CHAPTER NINE

Nanjing, Jiangsu

Noon, December 14, 1937

Shimada orders the driver to pull up outside the university. Hill gets out, but Shimada stops Lily by placing a hand on her arm. "You must be extremely careful. These are dangerous times."

"If you are Chinese," Lily can't stop herself from saying.

"Not just if you are Chinese," Shimada replies. "The Japanese army is immensely powerful, especially here in China, where we are a long way from the politicians in Tokyo. If Colonel Masao thought it would benefit the army, he would shoot me as readily as he would your friend Hill or the men by the river."

Lily looks at this small bookish man who is telling her he is in as much danger as she is. She doesn't believe him, but she does realize what a brave thing he has done in saving Hill.

"It was courageous and kind of you to help me rescue Hill. I don't know how I can thank you."

Shimada blinks rapidly behind his thick glasses. A smile spreads across his face, and he licks his lips. "Perhaps there is a way."

"What?" Lily asks, but even as she says it, realization grows in her. It sends a chill down her spine.

"We can discuss this some other time," Shimada says, glancing at Hill, who is watching them from a few feet away. "I am looking forward to the rehearsal of the play this afternoon."

"I'm sure you'll enjoy it," Lily says hurriedly as she climbs out of the car and joins Hill. They watch as the car drives off.

The snow is falling steadily as they trudge across the campus. It is only noon, but they both feel as if they have already lived through an eternity.

"What did Shimada say to you?" Hill asks.

"He just asked about the rehearsal later today."

"Thank you," Hill says. "That was quick thinking to go and get him. You saved my life. I was convinced I was about to die. I can't believe I'm not just one more corpse on the riverbank."

Now that they are safely back at the university, the enormity of the horror she witnessed overwhelms Lily. Her legs go weak, and she stumbles. Hill grabs her arms and pulls her close to him. Lily buries her face in his shoulder and sobs.

When the tears stop, she lifts her head and whispers, "I can't believe what I saw. All those bodies on the riverbank! I thought they were rocks when I first saw them. And the faces of the soldiers inside the fence—they were blank, expressionless. But the worst thing was the silence. No one shouted out or cried or argued or protested. It was as if they were already dead. Is it really true? Are all those people being systematically slaughtered?"

Hill nods. "It's true. They had already taken four groups to the beach before you and Shimada arrived."

"Why did no one try to escape? There must have been two or three thousand in the compound, and many of them were soldiers. They could have overwhelmed the guards. Some might have escaped."

"To what? To be hunted down later and used for bayonet practice? The Japanese are everywhere. The soldiers inside that fence have been fighting and losing for many weeks. They're starving and exhausted. All hope has left them. They are as helpless as wooden puppets being manipulated by forces much more powerful than they are. All that is left for them is to respond when the strings are pulled—even if the strings are leading them to death."

"Is this what humanity has come to?" Lily asks, gazing up at Hill. "Hopelessness and death? Just yesterday I was telling Neil that he, as an American, wasn't able to understand the harshness of life here. I thought I understood it, but I was wrong. The barbarity I witnessed this morning will haunt me for the rest of my days."

Hill leans forward and kisses Lily on the lips. It's not sexual. It's simply an acknowledgment of all they've shared.

When they draw apart, Hill says, "We will survive, whatever it takes. In a tiger hunt, no one notices the mice hiding behind the rocks. We will be like those mice. No one will notice us, and when the hunt has passed, we'll come out from behind our rocks and begin to live again."

As he talks, Hill leads Lily toward the theater. "But there is something we must do before we hide behind the rocks. Shimada told us the Japanese are planning a sweep of the university—perhaps as soon as this afternoon."

"Chen and the wounded soldiers in the boiler room!" Lily says, life returning to her voice.

"Exactly. They cannot escape in daylight, and if they stay they'll surely be discovered. They will be shot, we will be shot, and the Safety Zone will be closed."

"What can we do?"

Hill shrugs. "I don't know, but we have to think of something soon. The Japanese could show up at any moment. We can't count on them not coming until tomorrow. Is there any better place to hide the soldiers?"

"Twelve wounded men? I can't think of anywhere the Japanese won't search." Lily's brow furrows as she thinks. "But maybe the mice don't need to hide behind rocks."

"What do you mean?"

Suddenly Lily is all energy. "We need to talk to Neil. Where is he?"

"He was going to collect clothes for the soldiers."

"He must have finished that by now. He's probably preparing for the dress rehearsal. Come on."

Confused, Hill follows Lily as she hurries to the theater. Sure enough, Peterson is sitting on the edge of the stage, thumbing through the script for the play. He looks up as they enter.

"Where have you been?"

"It's a long story, Neil," Lily says as she strides forward. "I'll tell you later. Right now we have a more urgent issue. Shimada told us the Japanese are planning a sweep of the university."

"Good God. When?"

"Maybe this afternoon."

Peterson jumps down from the stage and begins pacing nervously. "They'll find the soldiers in the boiler room. I took civilian clothes down to them, but it won't hide the fact that they're soldiers. They have to leave. Now."

"It's the middle of the day," Hill points out. "They can't leave now. There are Japanese patrols all over. If they're caught in the Safety Zone, or even nearby, the Japanese will use it as an excuse to clear the zone. The effect will be the same as if they are found in the boiler room."

"Then we have to tell the Japs they're here. Perhaps if we show that we're cooperating and upholding the agreement, they won't close the zone."

Hill and Lily stare at Peterson, who continues his restless pacing, all the while rubbing his hands together anxiously. Their silence forces him to stop and look up.

"What?" he asks.

Lily takes a step forward. Her voice is edged with anger. "Are you suggesting we hand Chen and the others over to the Japanese? They'll be dead half an hour later."

"Don't be so dramatic. They'll be prisoners, yes, but they're soldiers defeated in battle—it's their lot to be prisoners of war. We have to take the larger perspective. The only way we can preserve the Safety Zone is to cooperate with the Japs and stick to the agreement that was made when the zone was set up. Which included not allowing soldiers in."

Hill pushes past Lily and advances on Peterson, his fists clenched. Peterson stands his ground, and the two face off toe-to-toe.

"You cowardly bastard," Hill hisses. "You would sacrifice my brother and his comrades for your own miserable life? And why not? They're only a rabble of dirty Chinese, right? You're a privileged American, entitled to pronounce godlike judgments on lesser mortals. Even the Nazi John Rabe is risking his life to help those around him. How will you be able to sleep tonight knowing that my brother was beheaded so some officer could test the sharpness of his sword?"

"Don't be ridiculous, Hill." Peterson's voice is infuriatingly calm. "That's not going to happen. And we must take the larger view. There are a quarter of a million lives at stake. We have to think of—"

Peterson's rationalization is cut short by Hill's fist striking him on the side of his head. The blow is wild and weakened by the fact that Hill has to swing up at the taller man, but Peterson jerks back a couple of steps and lifts his hand to his cheek.

Lily grabs Hill by the shoulders and pulls him back before he can swing again. He doesn't resist.

"Don't be stupid!" she scolds. "We're in the middle of a war against the Japanese and now you're fighting among yourselves?"

"It's not *his* war," Hill spits out bitterly. "He's an American. He can go home."

"Be quiet, Hill," Lily orders. "We've got more important things to discuss than your dislike of Americans."

"Thank you for calming him down," Peterson says, stepping forward and placing his hand on Lily's shoulder.

She shrugs him off. "You're as bad as he is. You think we live in a civilized world. We don't. We are in the midst of a barbarity you cannot imagine. Hill is right—Chen and the others will be executed as soon as the Japanese have them."

"But—"

"No buts, Neil. I saw things this morning I'll never forget. There's an evil at large here that is so vast we can barely comprehend it, and it leaves us only two choices—we can accept the horror and cower like mice behind a rock, or we can do something, however small, to fight against it. I believe that only by fighting—even if we have no chance of winning—do we retain our humanity. Wasn't it one of your philosophers who said that the only thing necessary for evil to triumph is for good men to do nothing?"

"From what you say, evil has already triumphed. We can't do anything to change that."

"We must do something," Lily insists. "Look, you said you chose to stay here because you wanted to experience life. But all you do is watch. To experience life you have to be *part* of it.

Maybe there's not much we can do, but that doesn't mean we should do nothing—that would make us as bad as the men with guns and swords."

Peterson stands immobile, staring at Lily. He thinks he has never seen anything so beautiful as her wide-eyed determination, but he's also terrified. The world he's being asked to experience is far more brutal than he'd expected. The civilization he imagined is dead in the ruins of Nanjing. He *is* an outsider, a sheltered observer protected by his American citizenship. He wants to experience life to inform his playwriting, but there's no point in experiencing life if you don't survive to use what you see. Perhaps Hill is right. Perhaps his rationalizations do hide a sense of racial superiority. Perhaps he is just trying to find a way to save himself.

He shifts his gaze to Hill, whose face is still angry. "Okay, I accept what you say in principle, but what can we do? There's no point in the mice jumping on top of the rock and shouting, 'Here we are! Come and kill us!'"

"I have a plan," Lily says.

CHAPTER TEN

Ashford, Ohio

Present Day

With his usual compulsiveness, Tone threw himself into his new role as actor. He took books on the theater and drama theory out of the library. He searched the Internet for lesser-known aspects of the Nanjing Massacre, including the involvement of foreigners in creating the Safety Zone inside the city. He watched movies, including one filmed secretly in 1937, and read all of Peterson's plays. He even talked to Pike about the historical research his friend had been doing in the depths of the university library.

Tone found his investigations strangely satisfying and a welcome change from the last bit of work on his thesis. He began to settle more comfortably into readings of *The Third Act*, and he felt he was beginning to inhabit the character of Hill. He was surprised to discover that he enjoyed standing in front of a mirror, pretending he was Hill. Even Pike's joking derision when he caught Tone at it didn't offend him.

The dark side of it all was Allen Quigley. The endless attention he paid to Theresa enraged Tone, and the asshole also seemed to go out of his way to belittle Tone. He took great pleasure in peppering his conversation with theater references he knew Tone wouldn't understand and then condescendingly explaining them to him.

On top of this, Tone's hope that his work on the play would bring him and Theresa closer wasn't panning out. She was totally absorbed in all aspects of the production, from the set design and costumes to mentoring the less experienced actors. Tone hardly saw her except when they were on the stage together. She continued to refuse all his requests to return to the house.

After a few days of read-throughs Quigley called a meeting of the principal performers and stage crew in an empty meeting room.

"All is going well," he began when everyone was settled around the table. "We've pretty well got the cast in place, and the sets and costumes are progressing"—he turned to Theresa—"mainly thanks to Theresa here, who seems to have more hours in her day than the rest of us."

Tone, who was sitting beside her, forced himself not to show his annoyance. To his mind, Theresa and Quigley were spending way too much time in each other's company. He knew it was inevitable—they were the two people most responsible for the production—but he still had to fight down his jealousy.

"And Tone—wow!" Quigley said, shifting his gaze. "I have to say, your performances improve exponentially with each rehearsal. Initially, I thought that if you could master the great Noel Coward's advice to know your lines and not bump into the furniture, you'd be doing well, but you have far exceeded that. In fact, I seriously believe you were born for drama. I think it a pity that you chose physics."

Tone composed his features to hide his emotions. What he wanted to do was tell Quigley off for being such a patronizing prick. What he did was smile and say, "Thank you, Allen. I really appreciate the chance you've given me. I think I have found a resonance with Hill, perhaps because he was Chinese. When I'm playing him, I can relate to the struggles he faced in such a tragic time in our nation's history."

Quigley gave Tone a small, insincere smile and turned his attention back to the group. "Gord, where are we at on promotion?"

"The playbills are printed."

Gord held up a glossy sheet. It was a collage of historical photographs from the Nanjing Massacre superimposed on the ghostly image of Peterson's face. At the top blood-red writing announced, *The Third Act: The Mystery of Neil Peterson's Unfinished Masterpiece. By Allen Quigley*. Smaller writing at the bottom gave the location and dates of the performances.

"Over the next day or two we'll be papering the campus—the whole town, in fact—with these. If any of you want a pile to hand out, just let me know. Also, I'm contacting the local TV and radio stations. The local paper will be sending someone to take shots of the lead actors in costume in a day or two, and there'll be reporters on opening night."

"Excellent," Quigley said. "And recruiting extras? How's that coming along?"

"Good. Obviously, since the play's set in China, I've been focusing on finding Chinese students to fill the stage in the crowd scenes. The response has been terrific. Most have never heard of Peterson, but they all know about the Nanjing Massacre and are happy to help a project that will make Americans more aware of Chinese history."

Gord hesitated for a moment before continuing. "One thing isn't working out so well, however. I thought it would be cool to have Shimada and the Japanese soldiers played by Japanese students. Problem is, there aren't a lot of Japanese students at Eastern, and the few there are know very little about the background. One guy I approached even denied that the massacre ever happened. He accused me of spreading anti-Japanese lies and propaganda. It was nasty. I thought we were going to get into a fistfight."

"No big deal," Quigley said. "Most of us here in America can't tell the difference anyway."

There was a moment of embarrassed silence around the table before Tone said, "Interesting, Allen. I've always thought you looked a bit pale for a Mexican."

Several people struggled and failed to suppress laughter.

"What?" Quigley said.

"Nothing," Tone said. "Just an observation."

"Uh, okay," he replied uncertainly. Then, after glancing down at his sheet of notes, he said with more conviction, "Gord, how are set construction and wardrobe coming along?"

"As you know, Allen, we're going with minimalist sets, but Theresa's doing a wonderful job of collecting archival photographs that we can project on the screen at the back. It'll save us from long set changes or having to paint complex backdrops. She's also searched out costumes and props I didn't know existed, so we're in good shape. Anything we can't find, we can wing it."

"Excellent," Quigley said. "Keep up the good work. Now, all of you, remember to invite some friends to the dress rehearsal. It'll give us a sympathetic audience for our final run-through before opening night." He stood up. "I think we're done here. Go and get some well-earned rest. Theresa, can you stay for a while?"

With much dragging of chairs, the room emptied.

"Can I borrow Theresa for a bit?" Tone asked.

"Strange way of putting it, Tone," Quigley said, "but of course you can. I don't control Theresa— in fact, I doubt if anybody could."

Tone and Theresa moved out into the corridor.

"Quigley really gets on my nerves," Tone said. "The way he dismissed Gord's fight with that asshole Japanese student! Doesn't he appreciate the tension between us and the Japanese over the Nanjing Massacre?"

"I'm sure he does. He's very sensitive. I think he's just so wrapped up in the details at the moment that he sometimes forgets the bigger picture."

"Would he have forgotten the bigger picture if it had been some neo-Nazi denying that the Holocaust ever happened?"

"It's not the same thing, Tone."

"No? Because we're outsiders here? Because Americans can't tell the difference between Asians? Because Hollywood thinks Chinese, Koreans and Japanese are interchangeable?"

Theresa stared at him long enough to make him feel uncomfortable. He hadn't intended to go on a rant about Quigley. Her brow was furrowed, and she looked concerned.

"But that's not what I wanted to talk to you about." He took a deep breath and let it out slowly. "Theresa, is there a problem between us?"

She looked thoughtful for a moment and then said, "You're right. To the Americans we're all the same. There are hundreds of Chinese students at Eastern. We come from all over the country and from a dozen diverse cultures. We speak different dialects and divide ourselves into groups, depending on the province or town we come from. But no one else sees that. They only see a throng of Chinese, all looking the same and talking a strange, incomprehensible language."

Tone was glad Theresa agreed with him, but he wondered where the conversation was going.

"When I first came over here, I was part of the crowd. I thought it was normal. The food in the cafeteria was strange and not very good, and I felt isolated because my English wasn't too good back then. But I worked hard at learning to speak and write the language well. I went out of my way to have conversations with American and European students. Even though I still hung out with Chinese students occasionally, I thought I was culturally assimilated. When you and

I met, and I started to spend more time with you and Pike, I didn't see it as a retreat. I thought we'd all assimilated in our own ways."

Theresa turned and stared out the window at the end of the corridor. "The other day Allen asked me why I chose to come to America. I was flippant. I told him it had seemed like a good idea at the time. That everyone else had come to 'Gold Mountain'—our ancestors who worked the mines and the railways—so I came too. But then I thought about it more. I thought about Peterson going the other way. Leaving his home and his culture to go to China in the middle of a war because he loved the plays of Guan Hanqing. He made a choice and risked his life for his passion. That's beautiful and romantic.

"And then I thought how that compared with my reasons. Did I—did most of us—come here for passion? No, we came for weak reasons—to get an education, to make money and be successful. We came because our parents expected us to or, as I told Allen, because everyone else was coming." She turned toward him. "You're different. You came here for passion. You came here for your love of science, physics, cryogenics, but for Pike and me, there's no passion. Our reasons are shallow. It's hard, and we put up with losing our culture for money or a hobby."

"Many people travel and live in other countries now," Tone said feebly. "It's a global world."

"But it's not the same for Americans. Something else Allen said made me think. A few years ago he went on a trip to the Philippines. He lived there for almost a year."

"My point exactly. He went to live in a very different culture. He didn't lose his."

"No, he didn't. But that's because he's American. He took his culture with him."

Tone frowned, trying to understand.

"For that year in the Philippines," Theresa explained, "everyone spoke English to Allen, or tried to. Many of the TV shows came from America or were in English. The shops sold American designer clothes—which, ironically, were manufactured in China. The hotel rooms were identical to those in Chicago or Denver. Every block had its McDonald's or KFC. Allen could live for a year in the Philippines without ever leaving home. And that applies to most places in the world if you're American. For God's sake, girls in Manila would come up to Allen and tell him he looked like Robert Pattinson."

"I see what you're saying," Tone acknowledged, "but where are you going with this?"

She stepped forward and gave him a hug. "I don't want to lose my culture. I've already lost my family. I know nothing of my grandparents or my father. My mother was one of the lost generation of the Cultural Revolution. She couldn't tell me anything about her family history and background—maybe that's why she was distant, emotionally unavailable. My father was a government official who either died or disappeared. I don't even remember him. Anyway, I thought coming to America would give me something meaningful, but it's only cast me further adrift. When *The Third Act* finishes its run,

I'm not going to MIT or California—I'm going back to China. I'm going home, Tone."

Leaving him dumbstruck, she strode back toward the meeting room. In the doorway, she turned and looked at him.

"I'm sorry," she said and closed the door.

Tone remembered nothing of going back to the house. He felt totally lost and alone, his mind a black fog of misery and self-pity. People swore and complained as he bumped into them, but he ignored them. All he wanted to do was get home. Maybe it was all a misunderstanding or some horrible nightmare, and he'd find Theresa sitting on his bed waiting for him. He was barely aware that he'd hauled his perfectly knotted tie loose. Barely aware of the tears streaming down his cheeks.

When he stumbled into the house Tone stood by the open door and looked around vacantly, as if not certain where he was or why.

Pike looked up from his book. "Shit, man. What happened to you?"

Tone blinked hard. "Theresa..." he croaked.

Pike stood. He put his arm around Tone's shoulders and led him back to the couch. "You need a drink, man. Stay there."

He went to the kitchen and rummaged noisily in the cupboards until he found a half-empty bottle of cheap Scotch left over from the last party. He poured a large shot into the cleanest glass he could find. He thought for a minute and then poured a smaller one into a second glass before returning to the living room.

Pike turned off the TV and handed Tone the bigger drink. His friend took a large gulp and coughed. Pike sipped his drink and asked, "So what's happened? Is Theresa all right?"

Tone sighed and took a second gulp. "All right? Yeah, she's all right." He rubbed his eyes and looked at Pike. "You were wrong the other day when you said Theresa thought going to MIT was great. She's not coming with me. She says she's going back to China."

"Wow," Pike said, then took another drink. He couldn't think of anything to say except "I'm sorry."

Tone drained his glass and carefully placed it on the end table among the empty beer cans. Pike expected him to start crying again, but instead he clenched his fists and stared at the carpet. Then he began beating his fists against his knees and muttering, "Shit!" under his breath.

Pike gave him a minute and then put an arm around his friend's shoulders. Tone stopped hitting himself and looked up. His eyes were dry and narrowed with hate.

"It's that bastard Quigley," he said. "Everything was fine until Theresa got the role in his damn play."

Pike didn't say anything.

"He put the idea of going home in her head." Tone was almost spitting. "She almost admitted as much. Him and his stupid play. I'll kill the bastard!"

"No, you won't," Pike said firmly. "Look, I know you're mad, and I know Quigley's an arrogant asshole, but give Theresa some credit. She's a strong person. She's not easily swayed by anyone—least of all someone like Quigley. If she's chosen to go back to China, it was her decision and no one else's."

Tone stared hard at Pike, as if trying to understand what he was saying.

"Look, you know how tough it is being Chinese and coming to America," Pike continued. "It's hard for everyone, and we adjust to the stress in our own ways. We'd all like to go home, but all kinds of pressures keep us here. Whether they're from family in China or ourselves doesn't really matter. We all try to find somewhere safe—a refuge. You take refuge in your work. I take refuge in partying. Maybe Theresa's the most honest of us all—she faces up to it and refuses to take refuge."

"You think so?"

"I know so."

Tone unclenched his fists and passed a hand over his face. "I felt so alone on my way back here. All I wanted to do was curl up into a ball and disappear. I thought it would all be so perfect. Theresa and I would go MIT and California and..." Tone trailed off, at a loss for words.

"Live happily ever after?" Pike suggested.

Tone managed a weak smile. "I guess that's part of the fake American dream too."

"Look, Tone, nothing lasts forever—especially relationships. You'll go to MIT and meet somebody else. Some total physics geek who you can talk to about things no one else understands."

"You're probably right, Pike, but I'm not ready to hear that yet. I do have MIT to hold on to though. If I didn't have that I don't know what I'd do."

"That's it! Focus on the positives. Time heals, et cetera, et cetera." Pike fell silent for a minute. Then he grinned and said, "Okay, I got nothing left. Let's go to the Blue Bar and get wasted. Are you up for working our way through every blue drink in the place?"

"I don't know about that, but I'm up for watching you try." Tone leaned over and embraced him. "Thank you, Pike. You're a good friend."

Pike hugged back briefly and pulled away. "Enough. Don't go all soppy on me, man. Look, I've got an idea of what we can do before we hit the bar. I guarantee it'll release some tension and take your mind off everything else."

"What?" Tone looked uncertain.

"If I told you, it wouldn't be a surprise, would it? Come on."

The pair walked outside, and Pike tossed the car keys to Tone.

"You're driving," he said.

"You're letting me drive your precious WRX? I don't even know where we're going."

"No sweat. I'll give you directions." He smiled at Tone. "I thought you liked being in control."

Tone hesitated and then returned the smile. "Yeah. Let's go."

As they drove through town, Tone relaxed and eased the speed up. Between giving him directions, Pike was talking quietly into his cell phone. Then they were heading out along East Road, and Tone allowed himself to open up the car a bit more. It felt good, and he was almost sorry when Pike directed him into the parking lot of the Gentlemen's Sport and Game Club.

"Why'd we come here? I didn't even bring the revolver."

"You won't need it. I've set up something special."

"This is going to cost you, man," Morrison said by way of welcome. "When you called I was just about to close up."

Pike pulled a wad of notes out of his pocket and threw them on the counter. Morrison regarded the cash for a moment.

"All right then," he said. "So, boys, what'll it be?"

"It's for my buddy here," Pike said. "I'm thinking something classic."

"We got a collection—Uzi, Thompson, Sten, MP40, maybe an FN, or everybody's favorite, the reliable old Kalashnikov AK-47. Your choice."

"They're all machine guns," Tone said. "I can't fire them on your range."

"Got a special range for these babies," Morrison replied with a smile. "Out back in the woods." He looked out the shop window. "Reckon you've got a half hour—maybe forty-five minutes—before dark. Better make up your mind quick."

"AK-47," Tone said without hesitation.

Morrison locked and bolted the metal front door, then led Tone and Pike through to a back room. The walls of the room were lined with gun racks. Every gun Tone had ever imagined was here. Morrison took down an AK-47 and showed it to Tone. "Pretty simple to use. That's the attraction—any idiot in a godforsaken jungle can blow holes in any other idiot without too much training."

Morrison ran through the basics of using it, then slid open a drawer and grabbed one of the curved magazines. "Clips in like this." The magazine snapped into place with a satisfying click. "To remove it, just push this button and twist it the opposite way." He removed the loaded clip. "Thirty shots each, and sturdy. Story is that Russian soldiers used them to open beer bottles."

He grabbed several magazines, tossed them into a faded leather shoulder bag and handed it to Pike. "You follow along behind and feed him fresh magazines. You're done when these are done. You got it?" Tone and Pike both nodded. "And you'll need these." Morrison gave them both wax earplugs. "It can get noisy out there."

Tone and Pike stuffed the plugs in their ears. They could still hear, but the noises were deadened as if by a pillow.

"Okay then," Morrison said, handing the AK-47 to Tone. "Let's get you started."

Even though it was unloaded, Tone felt incredibly powerful walking behind Morrison with the gun cradled in his arm. He could do anything. Theresa, Quigley, Seeger—no one else mattered. *He* was in charge.

Morrison led them out a back door and into the woods. A large irregular area had been partly cleared. Through it ran a twisting path surrounded by painted silhouettes. Some were simple outlines, while others represented soldiers in full camouflage gear.

"This is the outdoor range," Morrison explained. "Just follow the path and pick your targets—near or far, in the open or partly hidden. Whatever takes your fancy. Take your time." Morrison laughed. "It's not as if they're going to shoot back."

He disappeared back through the doorway. Tone stepped forward onto the path, and Pike handed him a magazine.

"Go for it, man," he said. "I'll be right behind you with refills."

Tone attached the magazine as Morrison had shown him and walked forward. To his right, about twenty paces away, he could see the crude outline of a head and torso above a bush. He cocked the weapon, pushed the lever down to the semiautomatic position, aimed and squeezed the trigger. Through the earplugs, the shot sounded like little more than a distant pop. A sliver of wood flew up from the figure's right shoulder. Tone adjusted his aim. The next three shots hit near the center of the torso. He adjusted again and fired until he could hit the head. Then he moved forward and repeated the process with a more distant figure.

As they progressed Tone's feeling of being in control increased. His face became set and expressionless as he practiced different shots at different ranges. A coldness came over him. The shooting became more than a game, the targets more than pieces of wood. Occasionally Pike made comments, but Tone ignored him. With each target, he fired one shot, adjusted his aim and then fired three or four shots in a cluster.

Tone became more obsessed as he worked his way through the magazines. With the more distant targets, he concentrated on hitting the torso, but with the closer ones he aimed for the head or a leg or an arm. Some of the close targets bore crudely painted faces. With them, Tone deliberately aimed for an eye. He found himself grunting with satisfaction when he hit his intended target and cursing under his breath when he missed.

The light was fading when Morrison shouted from the building, "We're going to have to close it down."

Tone didn't even hear him. He continued to shoot methodically at the targets, dropping each magazine on the ground when it was empty and reaching back for Pike to hand him a fresh one.

"Did you hear what Morrison said?" Pike shouted the next time Tone was ready for a refill. "We've gotta call it a day. It's getting dark, and anyway there's only one magazine left."

Pike had to repeat himself three times, but at last Tone turned around, his hand still outstretched. The tendons in his neck and the muscles of his jaw were bulging. His eyes were wide but icy, without emotion.

"Jesus, Tone," Pike said. "You're scaring me."

Tone didn't move. He just stood and stared until Pike placed the last magazine in his hand. Still staring coldly at his friend, Tone clipped the magazine in place, pulled the charger handle and flipped the lever to fully automatic. For an instant Pike thought, He's going to kill me. Then Tone turned away and stepped off the path.

"Hey!" Morrison shouted. "Stay on the path."

Tone ignored him and took off toward the cutout of a soldier in a crouching run. When he was about ten paces away, he stopped, lowered the Kalashnikov to his waist and pulled the trigger. Thirty rounds left the gun in a continuous stream, and the head of the cutout disintegrated. Tone stood and watched as the last pieces of wood drifted down. The barrel of the gun was smoking and the grip was burning his hand, but he didn't care. All he could see was ragged space where the head had been—where all his worries, struggles and frustrations had been. He felt cleansed and free, and there was a broad smile on his face when he looked back at Pike.

The moment when he'd thought Tone was about to shoot him was still vivid in Pike's memory. He gulped loudly. "Shit, Tone. You okay?"

"Never better," he replied, walking briskly back toward the building.

Pike took a deep breath. "I don't know about you, but I sure as hell need a drink."

CHAPTER ELEVEN

Nanjing, Jiangsu

Afternoon, December 14, 1937

Lily goes ahead of the group, making sure they don't meet anyone on the way to the theater. Chen and Hill lead the soldiers. They shamble along mindlessly, dressed in assorted civilian clothes. Peterson follows several steps back, deep in thought.

In the theater, cast members are gathering for the dress rehearsal. Most are already in costume, taking a last look at their lines. The set is simple. In the middle, a chair covered in an embroidered cloth serves as a throne. Red and green drapes form a backdrop.

As the soldiers move hesitantly into the theater, the actors stop what they're doing and stare at them. Lily smiles and announces, "We have the extras to play Lord Guan's and Lu Su's soldiers. Yuan, where are you?"

A young girl carrying a large bundle of clothing steps out from behind the curtains. "I'm here."

"Here are our soldiers," Lily says, ushering Chen and the others forward. "Clean them up, cover their obvious wounds, and make them look as soldierly as possible. Give them each two headbands. They will wear the red when they are Lu Su's soldiers and the green when they are Lord Guan's."

"Okay." Yuan drops her pile of clothes and waves the newcomers up onto the stage and behind the curtains.

Lily holds Hill's brother back. "Chen, do you know the story of Hanqing's play *Lord Guan Goes to the Feast*?"

Chen shakes his head. "I haven't had much time to read plays recently."

"The story is simple, and you and your men need not know all the details. It's set eighteen hundred years ago, at the time of the Three Kingdoms. Lord Guan, who is the general for the Kingdom of Wu, is in charge of the province of Jingzhou. But Lu Su, the minister for the Kingdom of Shu, wants to capture the province. He invites Lord Guan and his men to a feast, intending to ambush and kill them, but Lord Guan turns up on his own, armed with only a single sword. By the strength of his will, he overcomes Lu Su and destroys his plan.

"The play is in four acts and set in three locations—Lu Su's headquarters, Lord Guan's headquarters and a hermit's hut. When the drapes at the back of the stage are red, we are in Lu Su's headquarters. When they're green, we're in Lord Guan's. And when the embroidery is removed from the throne to reveal a simple chair, we are in the hermit's hut. You and your men will play Lu Su's and Lord Guan's soldiers—hence the different-colored headbands. You will have no lines and will not be required to act. All you have to do is be a part of the scenery. Do you understand?"

Chen nods. "I think we can do that."

"Excellent. Now, you should probably go and see how Yuan is doing with the costumes. We don't have a lot, but as long as each of your soldiers has some piece of ancient-looking armor, it should work. No one is expecting a full opera production. And try to give the helmets to the men with head wounds."

Lily watches as Chen disappears behind the curtains. She turns to address the cast members, who still stand about, puzzled.

"These are refugees who have kindly volunteered to help us out with the play by acting as soldiers. That is all they are. Do you understand?" Heads nod around the stage. "Good. They have been through a lot, and they're not trained actors, so give them whatever help they need. Thank you."

As the actors gradually go back to their preparations, Lily turns to Hill. "Do you think it'll work?"

Hill smiles nervously. "It has to."

"This is insane." Peterson steps up beside them.

"The world has gone insane," Lily replies. "What else can we do but join it?"

"This madness will kill us all."

"Then we'll die without blood on our hands. Look, Neil, only yesterday you were waxing eloquent about how safe we were, about how the Japanese were civilized and how everything would be back to normal in a day or two. What Hill and I witnessed on the riverbank this morning destroys any hope that you were right. The cast list has been posted, and we must all play our roles. What those roles demand, if we are to retain a trace of humanity, is that we act honorably—that we don't let fear overwhelm us and push us into this pit of depravity surrounding us. That we don't let evil triumph. We must make our choices and live with the consequences, regardless of what those consequences are."

Peterson, Hill and the actors close enough to hear Lily stand in silence, staring at her.

Choking back emotion, Hill steps forward and embraces her. "Thank you for helping us make our decisions," he whispers.

Peterson shakes his head. Why is everyone so comfortable making a decision that could mean death for them all? Before anyone can say anything else, he turns and strides out of the theater.

Lord Guan: Do you hear my sword?

Lu Su: What does that mean?

Lord Guan: When first my sword was heard, I killed Wen Chou. The second time my sword was heard, I killed Cai Yang. Is it your turn? Who owns Jingzhou?

Lu Su: Jingzhou belongs to us.

Lord Guan (beginning to draw his sword): This sword is not ordinary. It is overpowering when it is angry. It has quaffed the blood of many enemies and cleaved the heads of generals. It is a dragon in its scabbard and a tiger between us. If you persist in asking for Jingzhou, I will release my sword. We are meeting as friends. Let there be no dispute between us.

Peterson and Shimada are sitting at the back of the theater, watching the dress rehearsal. It has gone well and is almost done. Hill and Lily stand at the edges of the stage, giving minor directions when needed. Lily is beside Chen and his men, who all wear red headbands. She whispers to Chen, and he gestures to the others. The soldiers struggle to their feet. One stumbles and has to be helped by his comrades.

Lord Guan (turning to look at the soldiers): Is this a trap? If so, then you shall be the first to be cut in two.

Lu Su: No trap. Soldiers, it is too late.

Lord Guan (sliding his sword fully back in its scabbard): That is good. I shall take my leave.

Chen and the others remove the red headbands and replace them with green.

Lord Guan: I see my men have come to meet me. Please, Lu Su, escort me to my boat. I thank you for your generosity. The feast has been most entertaining, but I would remind you that art and trickery cannot overcome my sword.

The cast members leave the stage, and Shimada stands and applauds. Hesitantly Peterson joins him.

"A fine production," Shimada says, "considering the circumstances. You have some excellent actors to work with. Both Lord Guan and Lu Su were most convincing."

"Thank you," Peterson says. "It has been a struggle with all that's been going on."

Shimada smiles. "I am certain it has. It seems you had some difficulties casting the soldiers. They appeared very nervous, and some seemed positively ill."

Peterson tenses. "Ahh, yes. Um…" He stumbles over his words. "We had to…um, they are refugees. We had to bring them in at the last minute."

"Always a difficult thing," Shimada says. He looks inquiringly at Peterson. "You have been preparing this play for some time. Did the original players drop out unexpectedly?"

"Yes." The theater suddenly feels very hot. Peterson can feel sweat breaking out on his forehead. "They left just the other day. They wished to be with their families in these troubled times." It sounds weak to Peterson, but he can't think of anything else to say.

"Completely understandable," Shimada says with a smile. "All of them resigned from the play at once?"

"Yes," Peterson says. "They must have been discussing it among themselves. Fortunately, none of them had speaking roles. Nevertheless, it was a bit of a panic to find replacements. We'll work with them tomorrow. They'll be better for the opening tomorrow afternoon."

"I am certain they will," Shimada says encouragingly. "And Colonel Masao is not an avid theatergoer. I doubt he will notice anything amiss."

"Colonel Masao?" Peterson can feel the sweat trickling down his neck. "I...I didn't invite Colonel Masao. I thought you would be attending alone."

"Oh, I'm sorry, my friend." Shimada places a hand on Peterson's shoulder. "Did I not mention that I had invited Masao and a few of his military colleagues? Only officers, of course. They have been through much, and I thought it would be a chance for them to relax for an hour or two. I did not think you would mind."

"Of course not. They're very welcome."

"Excellent. Excellent." Shimada smiles. "Of course, the difficulties they have been through in the past days have made Masao and the others—how shall I say?—a little nervous. One might even say suspicious."

Peterson swallows hard.

"Fighting within a city is an altogether unpleasant business. The stress is almost unimaginable to those of us who have never undertaken it. The fighting is at close quarters, often in confined spaces—narrow alleys and small rooms. One never knows who is lurking around the next corner or watching from behind a collapsed wall. Is there a fanatic with a grenade hiding a few feet away from you? Are you being observed over the sights of a rifle? Is the friend beside you about to be blown to pieces, or is a bullet about to smash through your ribs and explode your heart?"

Peterson stares at Shimada. What's the little man getting at? Why is this reserved, bespectacled academic describing people being blown up?

"Many of these things are the normal lot of a soldier in wartime," Shimada continues, "but what makes street fighting particularly dangerous is that one can never be certain who is a friend and who is an enemy. It is easy for a civilian to become a soldier and"—Shimada blinks behind his thick glasses—"for a soldier to become a civilian."

Peterson's stomach knots, and the burning bile rising in his throat makes him cough violently. His mouth fills with saliva, and he struggles not to throw up. His skin feels suddenly clammy, and the sweat on his body goes cold.

"Are you all right?" Shimada asks politely.

Peterson struggles to regain control. He takes out a handkerchief and wipes his mouth and forehead. "Yes, yes," he manages to force out. "With all that's been going on, I haven't been sleeping or eating well."

"You must look after yourself. Especially in these difficult times." Shimada nods in agreement with his own words. "Anyway, I was going to say that the stress of urban fighting against an enemy you cannot easily recognize can lead to regrettable—yet perfectly understandable—overreactions on the part of tired and frightened troops. We must all work, through clear communications, to ensure that there are as few misunderstandings as possible. I hope you will think of me as a friend, someone to whom you may come and talk if anything is weighing heavily on your mind."

All Peterson can do is nod. The thinly veiled threat hasn't escaped him, and his mind is screaming, *He knows about the soldiers!*

Showing no awareness of Peterson's inner turmoil, Shimada asks, "What are your plans once the play is over?"

The change of topic throws Peterson. "I suppose I will return to the States," he replies.

"I have heard there will be a gunboat going downriver the day after tomorrow."

"That's very soon."

"It is, but these are times when opportunities must be seized. Do you intend to invite the delightful Lily to accompany you?"

"What? I guess so. If she wants to come." Peterson feels overwhelmed. First the veiled threat, and now what seems to be an order to leave.

Shimada rubs his chin thoughtfully. "Of course, you realize that the visa situation is now different. Everything must be approved by the Japanese military."

"Colonel Masao?" Peterson asks. He's beginning to glimpse where this conversation is going.

"Indeed. In your case—an American citizen wishing to return home—I can foresee no difficulties. Lily's visa might prove more challenging." Peterson opens his mouth to say something, but Shimada speaks over him. "Not necessarily, of course—if the right people speak up for her."

"And the right people would be you?"

Shimada smiles and shrugs modestly. "I used to have some influence, but times have changed. The army is in charge now. I cannot ask Masao for another favor...unless I have something to offer him in return."

"What do you mean? A bribe?" But even as he speaks, the answer is forming in Peterson's mind.

"A bribe?" Shimada says in mock horror. "Such a crude term. No, no. I am thinking more of information that might be of use to Colonel Masao—something that might clarify a situation that could otherwise lead to unfortunate consequences. If I had such a thing, we might all get what we want."

Peterson is silent. What is there to say? He's being ordered to leave, and if Lily is to accompany him, his choice is clear. He's trapped.

As Peterson wrestles with his thoughts, Shimada stares at the empty stage. "A very powerful performance indeed," he says quietly. "Scenes and images stay in one's mind after the performance, as they do with all great works of art. In particular, I felt that Lord Guan delivered the closing lines of the play very strongly." He pauses for a moment, then recites, "*I would remind you that art and trickery cannot overcome my sword.*"

CHAPTER TWELVE

Ashford, Ohio

Present Day

Quigley peered through the stage curtains at the audience. He stepped back and said softly, “It’s only about one-third full. I had hoped for more.”

“It’s just a dress rehearsal,” Theresa pointed out.

“Tickets have gone well for the opening tomorrow,” Gord added. “We should have a full house.”

“Still,” Quigley said, “I would have liked a full house tonight as well.”

“Farmers are never happy with the weather, and actors are never happy with the audience,” Theresa said with a smile. “Two facts of life. It will be fine.”

The cast members milled around backstage, some silently mouthing their lines, others fiddling with their costumes. Only Tone, standing off to one side, showed no emotion. But his gaze drifted between Theresa and Quigley.

Theresa noticed him and stepped over. "You okay?" she asked, not sure whether she meant with their relationship or the play.

"Sure," he replied. "Why wouldn't I be?"

"First-performance-in-front-of-an-audience nerves?" Theresa suggested, deciding to focus on the play.

Tone shrugged. "I've memorized my lines and I know when to say them." He glanced over at Quigley. "I've been doing some background reading, and I've thought of a couple of ways to improve the play."

"It's a bit late," Theresa said. "We open tomorrow night."

"I just thought that—"

"Okay," Quigley interrupted, "everyone not in the opening scene, please head backstage now." He watched as people moved off and the opening-scene actors took their places. Then he parted the curtains and stepped forward. The curtains closed behind him, but his voice carried through. "I'd like to thank you all for giving up your Friday night and coming here. I know it's only a dress rehearsal, but having an audience makes a huge difference. It means we can spot our mistakes more easily, and that gives us work to do tomorrow, rewriting and learning new lines before opening night. Otherwise, we'd just sit around feeling nervous and probably drink too much."

When the laughter died down, Quigley continued. "As you probably know, you are sitting in the Neil Peterson Theater, and that makes this a special occasion. I've come up with a new theory about what constituted Peterson's defining moment as a playwright and a solution to the mystery of why he never managed to write the last act of his China play. I don't pretend to be anywhere close to the caliber of playwright Peterson was, but I have in my humble way finished his play for him. I hope you enjoy this evening and that you'll return to see the finished play on another night. Ladies and gentlemen, *The Third Act*."

To scattered applause, Quigley came back through the curtain and took his position for the opening scene. As the curtains parted, the house lights dimmed and the stage lights illuminated three figures—Quigley as Peterson, Theresa as Lily and Tone as Hill. A black-and-white image of ruined buildings was projected on the back screen.

For the next fifty minutes Pike, to his surprise, was enthralled. He wasn't a theatergoer, preferring the vivid, computer-generated imagery of movies and games, and he had never suspected that a few people dressed in not very good costumes in front of an obviously fake backdrop could hold his attention so completely. Not only that, but that they could also make him feel a whole range of emotions and care about their make-believe lives. Tone was so wrong when he had called this playacting.

Pike had learned a lot about the Nanjing Massacre from school and his secret reading in the library, but he had never understood what it was like for those involved. Much as he disliked Quigley, he had to admit that he'd created something extraordinary.

Quigley's Peterson was totally believable as the naïve young American who had come to China to study a centuries-old playwright, fallen in love and got caught up in the Japanese war. His performance captured Peterson's horror at the brutality around him and his agonizing decision to stay when most other Westerners fled. Most convincing were his scenes with Theresa, especially those when he expressed his love for her, and Pike wondered how much of that was only good acting.

Theresa's Lily, meanwhile, exuded a fragile, sensitive beauty that hid a core of steel. Her speech explaining why they had to risk their lives to protect the wounded Chinese soldiers from the Japanese almost brought tears to Pike's eyes, and her determination in the face of all the tragedy made him want to stand up and cheer.

Understandably, Tone's performance was the least polished of the three, yet he managed to bring a raw energy and passion to Hill that conveyed his sense of sadness at his unrequited love for Lily.

At the moving conclusion of the play Theresa embraced Quigley, and the house lights went up. From the front row, Pike led the audience in standing and applauding wildly. Quigley beckoned the rest of the cast onstage. They formed a line and bowed in acknowledgment. Everyone looked ecstatic except Tone, who stared straight ahead without emotion.

When the applause died down Quigley disengaged himself from the line and stepped forward to address the crowd.

"Thank you, on behalf of all of us. You have given us poor players the greatest compliment you can. It has made every moment of the hard work over the past few days and weeks worthwhile. And I hope you will take away a clearer vision of Neil Peterson and his brilliant work. Thank you again."

There was more applause, and then the theater emptied. Pike remained seated.

Quigley turned to address the cast. "Well done, every single one of you. Take the rest of the night off. We'll meet again tomorrow. There are a couple of very minor points I'd like to address before we officially open."

The cast dispersed to the dressing rooms, chattering happily. Only Quigley, Theresa and Tone remained.

"Theresa, my dear, what can I say? No surprise, but you were magnificent. Watching you onstage was like watching the Lily I have inside my head."

Theresa smiled. "Thank you, Allen. I wouldn't have been half as good without the material you gave us to work with."

Quigley smiled in acknowledgment. "And Tone, I was right. You're a natural and perfectly suited to play Hill."

"Anyone for the Blue Bar?" Pike interjected from his seat.

"I don't think so," Tone said, and everyone looked at him in surprise. "I think we need to talk."

"What about?" Quigley asked. He sounded wary.

"I think your play is seriously flawed."

"What do you mean?" Quigley asked. "You heard the applause. We've got a success on our hands."

"People will applaud a trained monkey doing tricks. Success is nothing unless there is true meaning behind it. Your play doesn't explain the mystery of *why* Peterson couldn't write the third act."

"Of course it does. Weren't you paying attention?" Quigley's voice rose as he became angry. He sounded defensive. "Peterson was scarred by what he saw in Nanjing. When Lily refused to go with him to the States, she gave him the sole responsibility of making the world understand what had gone on. The immensity of the task was too much. He could never complete it."

"I believe there's more to it than that."

Tone's calm, detached manner sent Quigley's anger to the next level. He leaned forward and yelled in Tone's face, "What the hell do you know about creativity and character motivation? You've never written an imaginative word in your life! You exist in a universe of numbers and equations! How dare you criticize *my* play!"

Pike stood up and Theresa took a step forward, both worried the two were about to come to blows. Tone remained icily calm. He even smiled as he wiped flecks of Quigley's spittle off his face.

"You turn Hill into the villain of the piece when you portray him as betraying the wounded soldiers to the Japanese in exchange for the protection of his family."

"Yes. So what?"

"He would never have done that. Hill was a true patriot. He would have died happily if he knew that his death moved

China one step closer to throwing out the Japanese. He would never have made a deal with the invaders simply to save himself or his family."

"You can't know that!" Quigley shouted. "You haven't read Peterson's papers and letters!"

"True," Tone said calmly. "But I did find something interesting in my research for this role you so kindly offered me. Actually, I cannot take credit for discovering this." Tone looked over at Pike. "My friend pointed me toward the key to Hill. He told me about a book he'd found by a Maoist soldier who was fighting the Japanese in the north of China in 1938 and 1939. It's a fascinating tale. The soldier had many extraordinary adventures. His life was even saved by the Canadian doctor Norman Bethune. But what interested me most was his mention of a man who appeared out of the desert and volunteered to fight. Apparently, this man had walked from Nanjing in his private version of the Long March and only wanted to kill Japanese." Tone paused dramatically. "That man's name was Hill Chao."

Quigley stared at Tone, then shook his head. "That doesn't mean it's the same Hill Chao."

"I can't prove it," Tone said. "But the timing and the fact that he came from Nanjing—these things are persuasive. And, of course, the name fits, and Hill is not a common Chinese name. I think it's very likely it was the same Hill Chao, and if so, I think it proves Hill wasn't the one who betrayed the wounded soldiers to the Japanese. A man who trekked the length of China to join the communists so he could keep fighting the Japanese would never have betrayed anyone to the enemy. The only explanation that makes sense is that your beloved Neil Peterson did the betraying. That's why he could never finish the play—guilt."

Pike was rooted to the spot, riveted. Theresa and Quigley both stared—Theresa thoughtful, Quigley angry.

Quigley finally broke the silence. "Okay, you've found a reference to someone who might or might not be the Hill Chao who was with Peterson. Good for you. But I've done the research on Peterson. I've read every surviving word he wrote. There's nothing there to support what you suggest. Neil Peterson was an honorable man caught in horrific circumstances."

"Of course there's nothing in his writing about the betrayal," Tone conceded. "But it's the only explanation that makes any sense. You were right when you said I'm not a playwright—I know nothing about creative writing and what you call character motivation. But I think I understand Peterson. He's like Pike, Theresa and me—he's an outsider, living in a strange culture that he can never fully understand or be a part of.

"Okay, he was passionate about Guan Hanqing's plays, but it was an intellectual passion. Peterson was an American, born and bred. Hanqing's plays couldn't possibly have resonated with him the way they would with a Chinese reader who understood the history and knew the stories and allusions Hanqing used in his work. It's like Shakespeare for me. I can enjoy the plays on one level, but not in the same way as someone who has grown up in English culture and knows Tudor history."

Tone transferred his gaze to Theresa. "Yes, Peterson fell in love with Lily and was probably devastated when she refused to come with him to America. But people get over broken love affairs." Theresa couldn't hold his steady stare and looked down at the floor.

Tone turned back to Quigley. "Peterson made the choice to stay because he wanted to live life to the full—because he believed it would inform his work and make him a great playwright. He saw much more than he bargained for, and it must have been devastating, but that's what he was there for—to experience life. And it *did* make him a great playwright. There was only one thing he couldn't write about: his own behavior."

"Shit," Theresa said under her breath.

"What?" Quigley asked. "Don't tell me you agree with him!"

"I don't know, Allen. It's an interesting theory, and guilt's a powerful motivator."

"There's absolutely no evidence for what you suggest," Quigley said. "Hill is the obvious betrayer. Peterson may never specifically accuse him, but he talks about the close relationship between Hill and Shimada, and how Shimada wanted Hill to go and study in Kyoto. Doesn't that strike you as odd in the middle of a war?"

Before Tone can respond, Quigley goes on. "Hill also had family in the city, and they needed protection. And Peterson does say that Hill left the Safety Zone in the middle of the night, before the soldiers were arrested. It would have been an extraordinary risk for any Chinese male to wander outside the Safety Zone while the massacre was going on. He would have been insane to do that unless he had some kind of Japanese protection. Protection he could have got for himself and his family by betraying the hidden Chinese soldiers."

"Or," Tone said, "he had some other compelling reason for his actions."

"Like what?"

"It could have been anything. Maybe he went out looking for food. Maybe someone else left the Safety Zone and he went after them. This far away in time, we can't know, but we have no proof that it was betrayal. You judge Peterson by American standards, and that's fair enough, but you can't apply the same standards to the Chinese. Peterson was safe in Nanjing. America and Japan had a treaty. That wasn't the case for Lily and Hill. Even in the Safety Zone, they—and especially Hill, because he was male and of military age—lived with the knowledge that at any minute they could be dragged down to the river and shot or bayoneted or, in Lily's case, much worse. The stress must have been unimaginable. How can we, this removed in time, possibly assign specific motivations to these people?"

"That's my point exactly," Quigley said. "We must interpret based on what *evidence* we have."

"And the soldier's diary is a crucial piece of new evidence." Tone crossed his arms. "I think my interpretation is more valid."

Tone and Quigley stood looking at each other, Tone relaxed, Quigley tense.

"Wow!" Pike said to break the tension. "I was brought up on bad movies with car chases and shootouts. I had no idea theater could be this interesting. This is even better than the play."

No one laughed.

"Okay," said Theresa, stepping forward. "You both have theories about what happened more than eighty years ago on the other side of the world. You've both put a lot of thought into this, and you each believe your theory is correct. But neither of you can prove anything. Maybe one day someone will find Peterson's lost diary or unearth some letters that Hill wrote or trace what happened to Lily after Peterson left, but nothing is going to be resolved tonight. And all of this is academic anyway, since we can't make a change of this scale before tomorrow night. So I suggest we all get a good night's sleep, work on polishing the details tomorrow and accept that the applause is going to be enough."

For a moment she thought Quigley was going to continue the argument. Instead he said, "Theresa's right. What you and Pike discovered does potentially change the interpretation, but there's nothing to be done before tomorrow."

Tone gave a strange smile and jumped off the stage. "Come on, Pike," he said, grabbing his friend's arm. "You said something about going for a drink."

"Sure. But you're still in costume, man."

Tone smiled. "Do you really think the clientele of the Blue Bar will object to someone dressed as a Chinese peasant from the last century?" He headed up the aisle.

"I guess not." Pike looked up at Theresa, raised his eyebrows and gave a small wave before following his friend out.

"The nerve of that guy," Quigley said. "He knows nothing about theater. I give him a chance, and he turns around and challenges me on a topic on which *I'm* the expert. I've spent months researching and writing this play."

"It's an awesome play, Allen," Theresa said, moving over beside him.

"Do you really think so?" Quigley looked like a small child whose teacher had just given him a D for a project he'd worked on for days.

"Of course I do. And so did the audience. They loved it."

"But do you think Tone's interpretation is better than mine? Do you think Peterson could have betrayed the soldiers, and that's why he never finished his play?"

Theresa could see that portraying Peterson as the betrayer would strengthen the play's ending and that guilt would have been a strong motivator for the real-life Peterson. But all she said was, "Everything that far back in time is open to interpretation. You've created a wonderful play that will be a great success. What more can any playwright wish for?"

"You're right." Quigley breathed a sigh of relief. "Thank you." He pulled Theresa to him in a hug, which she returned.

When he stepped back he said, "Let's go for a drink to celebrate."

"Okay, but on two conditions. One, we get out of costume first, and two, we don't go to the Blue Bar."

"Deal. I know the perfect place."

"Where are we going?" Theresa asked.

They were in Quigley's car, driving through a rundown part of town she'd never ventured into.

"It wouldn't be a surprise if I told you," Quigley replied. "Anyway, we're almost there."

She stared out the car window at the seedy walk-up apartments, the liquor and convenience stores with barred windows, and the tattoo parlors. "Not the best neighborhood," she remarked.

"Sure, there are problems, but that's because it's a poor neighborhood. Most of the people here are just the same as people everywhere, simply trying to get by. I like it because it's a mix of all sorts of people—African Americans, Hispanics, aging hippies. It gives the area vibrancy."

"Do you live around here?"

"No, I have an apartment in the high-rise downtown. It's way more dangerous than here."

"Really?"

"Sure. I'm on the seventeenth floor. The fire ladders only reach as far as the twelfth."

Theresa laughed. She was seeing a different side of Allen. He seemed more relaxed outside the theater. "Did Tone's theory about Peterson upset you?" she ventured.

Quigley drove for a block in silence before answering. "Honestly? Yes. A theater director has to be in charge, has to keep a lot of sometimes very flaky people on the same page. A playwright has a clear image of how his or her work should be presented, and it's difficult to see past that. With *The Third Act*, I'm both director and writer, so perhaps I'm overly sensitive." He smiled ruefully. "And Tone's timing wasn't great. Maybe if he'd come to me a week ago and talked it over, I'd have been more receptive. But throwing a radical idea out there at the last minute, when it's too late to do anything about it, was just asking for a knee-jerk reaction."

"Do you think there's any possibility that Peterson was the betrayer and that he spent the rest of his life wracked by guilt?"

"No. I've spent so long in Peterson's company I feel I know him really well. In a sense he's become my friend, and I can't see him as someone who would betray the wounded soldiers." He hesitated. "But then again, maybe I'm projecting. Maybe I want Peterson to be the hero because I admire him so much. Far too often we attribute aspects of a creator's work to the creator himself. That's why it's so devastating when a writer we admire turns out to be a wife beater or a pedophile or just plain creepy. Perhaps that's what I'm doing with Peterson."

He shrugged and glanced over at Theresa. "Regardless of his bad timing, Tone's ideas are certainly interesting. When the play's done, I'll go back over my research notes and read the diary he mentioned to see if I can find anything to support his theory."

"That's very generous of you."

"Generosity has nothing to do with it. One day I hope to turn *The Third Act* into a full-length play about that time in Peterson's life. I want it to be as accurate and powerful as possible. If Tone's idea can be supported, I'll use it."

"Tone's wound very tight right now, Allen. He has a brilliant mind, and not just in the field of physics. But when he works through a problem in his head, his answer is the only one. Truth is, it's usually the right answer. But he can't see that others may have different opinions and that they can't always be convinced of his arguments. He doesn't understand that controversial ideas have to be approached subtly. Tone thinks that once he's discovered an answer, all he needs to do is tell others—regardless of their feelings or whether the timing is appropriate."

"It comes across as very controlling."

"Absolutely, and it can make me furious. Sometimes I think Pike is the only person who doesn't get wound up by that side of Tone. He just lets the world and the people in it flow over him."

Quigley eased the car into the turn lane at a set of lights. A bearded man in filthy, mismatched clothes waved a ragged cardboard sign at him. The sign read *Homeless. Need Money for Food. Thank U.* Quigley rummaged in the console between the seats, hauled out a ten-dollar bill, lowered the window and held it out.

"Thanks, man," the guy said as he took the money.

The arrow flashed and Quigley pulled into a crowded parking lot in front of a wooden building with an illuminated sign announcing *Michael Collins House*.

"That was a nice thing to do," Theresa said, "but I doubt he'll spend the money on food."

"That's not the issue for me. He's obviously short of money. I made the decision to give him a little. As soon as I do that, the money's not mine anymore. How it's spent is his choice."

Theresa was impressed by Quigley's gesture. She wondered if Tone would have done the same.

As if reading her mind, Quigley asked, "Do you find Tone annoying?"

"Sometimes incredibly so. That's why I'm not going to MIT with him."

Quigley swiveled his head to look at her. "Are you staying here?" he asked, a bit too eagerly. "There will be opportunities in the theater after *The Third Act*. I've persuaded a few big names to attend tomorrow's opening night. Your performance will wow them."

"Thank you, Allen," she said with a smile. "But no, I won't be staying here. I'm going back to China. That's my home, and if I'm any good as an actress, I'll make a go of it wherever I end up. Besides, I want to try to find out what happened to the family I never had."

"I'm sorry you won't be staying here." He was unable to keep the disappointment out of his voice. "But you *will* be a star wherever you go."

"Enough! I can't take any more compliments." She waved her hands in the air and turned to look at the building across the parking lot. "Why are we here?"

"With all the talk about choices and cultural heritage, I thought I'd show you something of my heritage and the choices my ancestors made."

He exited the car and headed for the front door. Lights gleamed through every window of the building, and the sound of fiddles and drums drifted out into the evening. Intrigued, Theresa followed him inside.

Stepping into the entrance hall was like stepping back in time. Rich wood-paneled walls stretched up to a vaulted wooden ceiling. The walls were decorated with brightly colored armorial crests. To their right a wide staircase led up to the second floor, the wall beside it lined with large oil paintings of stern, bewhiskered old men. In front of them, a wide corridor stretched toward an archway that led to the source of the music.

Quigley showed a card to the doorman and had Theresa sign the visitors' book.

"A hundred years ago," Quigley explained as they strolled around looking at the paintings and coats of arms, "this was a mansion belonging to an Irishman who made a pile of money through some shady deals and questionable mining ventures. Although he never returned home, he became quite nostalgic about the land of his ancestors in his old age. He named the house after the Irish rebel hero Michael Collins, and he spent his money collecting paintings and old weapons. He had no family, so when he died he left money and provisions in his will for the house to be run 'for the benefit of all true and loyal Irishmen.' So now it's the Michael Collins Irish Benevolent Society House."

"I didn't know you were Irish. Is Quigley an Irish name?"

"To be sure, it is," Quigley said in a mock Irish accent. "I have it on good authority that it means 'untidy.' And here's my noble coat of arms." He pointed up at a crest that showed a bright red shield cut by a broad yellow diagonal band. Stylized plants twirled around the shield, which was topped by a medieval knight's helmet.

"A bit overdone," Theresa observed.

Quigley laughed. "It is. I doubt my ancestors in the bogs of Ireland cared much about this sort of thing. I suspect it has all been exaggerated for the tourists. Shall we get a drink?"

"That would be nice." She followed Quigley through to the hall at the back. "The whole place is made of wood," she said, gazing up at the ornate hammer-beam ceiling far above. As in the entranceway, the walls were wood-paneled and ornately decorated, this time with a collection of shields, axes, pikes and swords. "Warlike lot, your ancestors."

"I like to think we've mellowed over the centuries. What would you like to drink?"

"White wine, dry. Thank you."

While Quigley went to the long bar at one end of the room, Theresa found an empty table and looked around. On a low stage in front of a stone fireplace large enough to roast an ox, there was a five-person band playing Celtic reels. Two circles of dancers were performing complex steps.

Quigley returned with Theresa's wine and a whiskey for himself. He sat down and lifted his glass. "May you be in heaven half an hour before the devil knows you're dead."

Theresa furrowed her brow. "What on earth does that mean?"

"It's a traditional Irish toast," Quigley said with mock seriousness.

"Traditional or not," she said, clicking her glass against his, "here's to the man who finished Neil Peterson's play. May it end up on Broadway."

He smiled in acknowledgment. "With Theresa Li in the role of Lily," he added as they took a drink. "So I told you what my name means. Now you have to tell me what yours means."

"It's much more complicated than 'untidy.'"

"That's fine. I have plenty of time, and we have a bar and musical accompaniment."

She laughed. "The first recorded use of the name is Li Er, the founder of Taoism, in the fifth or sixth century BCE. But it didn't become popular until it was used by the emperors of the Tang Dynasty more than a thousand years ago. There are several legends about the origin of the name. My favorite is that at the end of the Shang Dynasty, a minister of the cruel king Zhou was murdered. His son escaped and survived by eating plums, so he changed his name to the Chinese character for plum, which is the same as the character for Li."

"And all I have is an untidy tribal chief. I think that calls for another drink."

Before Theresa could respond, Quigley was on his way to the bar.

"So I can't persuade you to stay and become a famous actress here?" he asked when he returned with two more drinks.

"My mind's made up," she said, sipping her wine. "I came here to study drama because I felt that Chinese theater was too restrictive. I thought it would be more flexible here, more open. I was wrong. It's just as restrictive here, only in a different way. I guess we can never truly escape our culture and heritage." She looked pointedly at the mock baronial hall and the Irish paraphernalia mounted on the walls. "I mean, here we sit, surrounded by your culture, listening to its music being played on authentic instruments." Her gaze rested on a musician working seriously on a set of small green bagpipes.

"They're uilleann pipes," Quigley said, following her stare, "but don't think I'm here for them. I'm not a huge fan of traditional Celtic music, or of the fourth- or fifth-generation Irish who come here and cry into their beer about how wonderful the homeland is. When the potato crop failed back in 1847, my ancestors had a choice: get on a coffin ship and try to survive the journey to the New World, or end up in a famine grave outside the village. Not much of a choice, really."

"And not one they could reverse."

"Indeed not, despite being hated, vilified and condemned to the lowest jobs by the culture they had come into. But then, very few choices are truly reversible."

"I'm reversing my choice to come here."

"You're not. You made a decision to come here, and that had consequences. You met Tone, Pike, me. You starred in *The Third Act*. And a thousand other things. They all changed you in subtle ways. The Theresa who has now decided to go back to China is not the Theresa who decided to come here. You're a different person, so they're different choices. If I chose to go back to Ireland, it wouldn't be the same choice my ancestors made to come here. You say you can't escape your culture, but you also can't escape the experiences that make you the person you are."

The band started a fast tune, and several people left their tables to dance. Quigley finished his drink.

"But we've had too much serious talk this evening." He stood up and held his hand out to her. "Let me show you the one really worthwhile talent my culture has. I'll teach you to dance."

Theresa wondered how she had ended up in Allen's bed. Certainly she'd drunk a couple of glasses of wine too many and danced until she was tired, but there hadn't been a moment when she'd thought, I'm going to have sex with Allen. They had simply gotten into his car, driven to his apartment and headed upstairs for a nightcap. They had kissed in the elevator and forgotten the nightcap.

Theresa rolled over and opened her eyes. Allen was lying on his back, breathing steadily. She studied his profile.

There was no denying that he was good-looking, in a classical Western sense. She was accustomed now to the looks of Western men, but his features still seemed too large, overcrowding his face.

She looked over at the window, where shafts of morning sunlight knifed in at the edges of the blinds. She thought about Tone. He and Allen were so different. Did she love him? Did she love *either* of them? The answer popped into her head surprisingly fast. No.

"Breakfast's almost ready."

Allen looked up as Theresa came into the kitchen, wearing one of Allen's collarless shirts. "Wow," he said. "That shirt looks a hell of a lot better on you than it does on me. There's fresh-squeezed orange juice on the table, and the coffee's percolating."

Theresa took a glass of juice and walked over to look out the picture window at the panoramic view of Ashford. Allen's apartment building was one of the few high-rises, and she had an uninterrupted view of downtown, the university and a swath of surrounding countryside. It was the first overview she'd had of the town, and her first impression was that it was incredibly clean. The morning air was clear and the buildings spotless. There were no factories belching dark pollution, no ramshackle slums hazy with the smoke from cooking fires. It looked like a perfect toy town, with everything in its appropriate place.

She knew from her drive with Allen the previous night that, at least in some parts of town, the perfection was an illusion. She wondered how she would readapt to the bustle and noise of her homeland—but maybe that was the point. Life *was* bustle, noise and messy confusion. To pretend otherwise was a lie or at best a pretense. Sooner or later—unless you had enough money to create your own little artificial island—the bustle and noise would intrude. Wasn't it better to accept that from the start, especially if you wanted to be an actor whose mission was to portray reality and all its complexity to an audience?

Theresa took a sip of her orange juice. In a way she understood Peterson's desire to go to China and his decision to stay in the middle of a war. Serious artists, whatever their discipline, had to experience life in order to express it. Unlike physicists, she thought, as her gaze drifted over the neighborhood where Tone and Pike lived. She wondered what Tone was doing this morning. If he'd gone to the Blue Bar with Pike after the rehearsal, he probably had another hangover.

Her thoughts darkened as she remembered Tone pointing that gun at her as she came through the bedroom door. No, that wasn't fair. He wasn't pointing the gun at her—he was just fooling around. But the memory still disturbed her. Tone had issues, including a tendency toward defensive rage when he was crossed or didn't get his way. How did a gun fit into that?

Theresa shook her head. She was being unreasonably hard on him, probably because she felt guilty about sleeping with Allen. In truth, Tone seemed to have gotten over her news that she was going back to China quite quickly, and he would never do anything stupid. Stupidity required spontaneity, and he was the least spontaneous person she knew. Still, she hoped nothing ever happened to push Tone to the edge. She suspected it was a big drop.

"Beautiful, isn't it?" Allen appeared beside her, holding two mugs of coffee. He passed her one.

Theresa smiled. "Worth living above the limit of the fire department's ladders."

He laughed. "Sometimes I stand here and feel like a god."

"Maybe that's not such a good idea," Theresa said. "'Kill one man, and you are a murderer. Kill millions of men, and you are a conqueror. Kill them all, and you are a god.'"

"That's pretty depressing. Where did you hear that?"

"Strangely enough, Tone told me. It's by a French philosopher and biologist called Jean Rostand. He worked on low-temperature stuff like Tone does, and apparently he influenced the guy who started the company that will freeze your body so you can be thawed out whenever a cure for what you died of is discovered."

"I should sign up for that," Allen said with a smile. "The future will need me. I doubt if I could afford it though."

"You could always do the cheapo option and just have your brain frozen."

"Now we're really getting into science-fiction territory. Come and have breakfast before *it* gets frozen."

He lifted her coffee mug from her hands and went to refill it while she made her way to the table. "This looks incredible," she said, taking in a perfectly arranged plate of eggs Benedict and fresh fruit. "Where did you learn to cook like this?"

"Entirely self-taught. From when I first started living on my own. I don't like pizza, McDonald's or takeout food, so I had to learn to cook in a hurry."

Allen handed her a mug of fresh coffee, sat down across the table, placed his chin in his hands and gazed at her thoughtfully. "You are incredibly beautiful," he said at last.

"You keep saying that," Theresa said, even though she felt herself blush.

"It's because it's true. Last night was special."

She shifted uncomfortably. "It was a lovely evening, and I appreciate your sharing your history and culture with me."

"Is that all?"

"Okay. I had a great time. But I *am* going back to China."

"Why? You have everything here."

"Maybe that's part of the problem. Things have worked out wonderfully for me here. It would be so easy for me to be seduced by that—beautiful Chinese girl leaves home and crosses the world to find adventure. She finds fortune and fame and...stops being Chinese."

Allen looked puzzled. "Is that wrong?"

"I don't know, but I can only find out by going back to China."

"Is it Tone?"

Theresa sighed. "No, it's not Tone. Why do men always think the only threat is another man?"

Allen looked like he wanted to protest, but Theresa waved him off.

"In the nineteenth century thousands of Chinese men came over to North America to work on the railways and in the mines," she said. "They called it Gold Mountain, and even though they were given the worst, most dangerous jobs to do and were paid a pittance compared to European workers, it was still more money than they could dream of making in China. They saved and they sent money home and they brought their families over, despite the head taxes that were brought in to stop them.

"But did they wonder if they'd done the right thing? Was it worth the prejudice they had to endure? They had no choice—just like your Irish ancestors who came over to escape the famine. The Chinese couldn't return to China any more than the Irish could go back to Ireland. Either they became Americans or they tried to recreate China in ghettos from San Diego to Vancouver. But I *do* have a choice. I can go back and see which place is right, which culture I want to belong to."

Allen looked distraught. "I love you, Theresa," he said softly. "Please stay with me."

She shook her head. "I can't stay with you, Allen. And you can't love me after only one night together. I'm fond of you, and I really do appreciate everything you've done for me, all the help you've given me, but would you ask me to give up centuries of my culture for that one night?"

"Yes," Allen said. "I would."

"Well, I'll do the same. Will you come to China with me? Will you give up your heritage and become Chinese, without any chance of coming back here? Because that's what you're asking me to do."

Allen covered his face with his hands. Theresa was afraid he was about to burst into tears. Instead he rubbed his eyes and looked up.

"You're right," he said. "It's not fair of me to ask that of you." He smiled weakly. "When I'm a famous playwright, will you come back and star in one of my plays?"

"Only if you write a strong Chinese character."

"I promise I will. And when you're the lead at the National Centre for the Performing Arts in Beijing, I'll be in the front row, cheering."

Theresa walked around the table and hugged Allen. "Thank you for understanding."

"I'm a playwright," he said with a smile. "I understand tragedy." He glanced at his watch and stood up. "But the real tragedy will be if we don't get over to the university and finish preparing for opening night."

CHAPTER THIRTEEN

Nanjing, Jiangsu

Afternoon, December 14, 1937

"What were you and Shimada talking about?" Lily and Hill emerge from behind the stage curtains and move beside Peterson, who sits dejectedly with his head in his hands.

Peterson looks up. "What? Oh, he was complimenting me—us—on the play."

"Is that all?" Hill asks. "You seemed deep in conversation for some time."

"He told me he's invited Colonel Masao and some other officers to the opening tomorrow."

Lily and Hill stare at him in horror.

"The Japanese army is coming to the performance?" Lily asks.

"Just Masao and a few officers," Peterson says weakly.

"Just Masao and a few officers!" Hill is almost yelling. "What have you done?"

"I've done nothing," Peterson snaps, standing to face Hill. "Shimada didn't tell me he was going to do it, and I could hardly say, 'Oh, sorry. Masao can't come because he might spot the soldiers we're hiding in the play.' Let me remind you that it wasn't my idea to bring them here or to put them in the play."

"Stop, both of you!" Lily says. "We all faced difficult choices, and we all made decisions we felt were right at the time. We have to live with that and move on. I, for one, am committed to saving these men's lives."

"Even if it means others will die?" Peterson asks.

"I am not responsible for what the Japanese will do if I fail."

"But you *must* look at the larger picture—the lives of the few against the lives of many."

"I'm sick of hearing that from you, Neil," Lily says. "It can be used to justify too much. There have to be absolutes we stand by regardless of the consequences."

"I will take my men out of the Safety Zone as soon as it gets dark." Chen has suddenly appeared.

"You can't," Hill says, turning to face his brother. "The Japanese are everywhere. You won't survive a day, and Lily and I have seen what happens to anyone suspected of being a soldier."

"We will split up. Some of us will make it."

"No, you can't leave," Peterson declares.

"What do you mean?" Hill asks. "You're the one who's been pushing for us to expel Chen and the others."

"Shimada wanted to know why we had these inexperienced extras. I told him the previous extras had all quit to go home."

Lily stares at Peterson, but he refuses to meet her eyes. "So we continue with the plan?"

"We have no choice," Hill says.

Chen bows to the others. "We are honored by your bravery. We shall attempt to become better actors by tomorrow."

"So we're all agreed?" Lily keeps her eyes on Peterson.

"The choices are made," Hill says. "Come on, Chen—we have work to do."

The brothers move down to the stage, leaving Peterson and Lily alone in the shadows.

"You've made your choice?" she asks.

"I have," Peterson says. He takes a deep breath and looks up. He seems so desolate that for an instant Lily is certain he's about to break down. Instead he says, "There's a gunboat heading downriver the day after tomorrow. Shimada suggested—in the strongest terms—that I get on it."

"And will you?"

He nods. "I want you to come with me."

Lily remains silent for a long time. Finally she says, "There was a time when I would have eagerly accepted what you offer, but times have changed."

"Is that a no?"

"It doesn't matter." She shakes her head. "It's impossible for me to come with you in two days' time. I could never get a visa that fast."

"If you had a visa, would you come?"

"That's a pointless question. I don't have a visa." She starts to move down the aisle toward the stage. "Whether you are on that gunboat or not, we have much to do before tomorrow afternoon."

She's relieved to be away from Peterson and his questions. She'd always assumed that when he returned to America, she would go with him. That's changed now, and not just because she has no visa. Peterson's unwillingness to protect Chen and the others has opened a gulf between them. It would feel like desertion if she went away with him.

Peterson watches Lily go. His belief that he can remain detached from what is going on around him seems to be disappearing into the shadows with her. Now all he wants to do is return to comfortable, familiar America, where he will no longer be trapped by moral dilemmas that have no easy solutions. He wants to escape—with Lily.

He clenches his fists. Maybe there is one choice he can make that will allow everything else to fall into place. He watches as Lily climbs onto the stage and begins talking to Hill, then shakes his head and strides out of the auditorium.

Lily looks up at the sound of the door closing. Peterson's seat is empty. "I'm worried about Neil," she says to Hill. "He seems to be right on the edge. I hope he's not going to do something stupid."

"Peterson's learning what the world's really like," Hill says. "It's not a pleasant process, but he'll survive. In the meantime, we have more important things to worry about.

We need to get the medicine and food for Chen and the others."

"You're right. I'll go to the hospital and look for bandages and medicine. You go and see what food you can collect."

"Okay. It'll be dark soon. I don't think the Japanese will do a sweep today, but in case they do, Chen and his men should stay in the theater. If anything happens, they can say they are rehearsing."

Lily nods as Hill goes to join Chen and the others. But she can't stop thinking about what Peterson might do.

The hospital is seriously overcrowded, but a nurse gives Lily a small sack of bandages, several gauze pads and a sling. They have no medicine to spare. As the twilight thickens on her way back to the university, Lily detours to avoid a squad of Japanese soldiers. Her new route takes her close to the Japanese embassy, and she's surprised to see Peterson ahead of her.

She's about to call out to him, but something about his furtive movements makes her hesitate. She follows and watches as someone steps out of the shadows. It takes Lily a moment to recognize the squat, bespectacled figure of Akira Shimada. As the two men fall into conversation, a Japanese soldier steps out from behind Shimada and looks around. Lily ducks into the doorway of an abandoned house. But she wants to know what Shimada and Peterson are talking about, so she works her way through the building to get as close to them as possible.

The house looks to have been elegant once, but the blast that blew in the windows and doors has tipped the furniture over and scattered broken glass and shattered ornaments across the patterned carpets. Heavy wallpaper hangs in forlorn strips, and gaping holes in the plaster reveal bands of wooden lath. Lily carefully moves to a room close to Shimada and Peterson, crouches beneath a broken window and listens.

"We have an understanding then," she hears Peterson say.

"Of course," Shimada answers. "In times like these we must help each other."

"You can guarantee a visa for Lily in time for the gunboat?"

"Of course," he repeats. "I will talk to Colonel Masao. With the information you have given me, there should be no problem. You have been a great help. Now you must go back to the university. It is not safe on the streets after dark, even in the Safety Zone, and I would hate for the world to lose such a promising playwright."

Lily risks peeking out the window. She sees Peterson nod and the two men shake hands. Peterson heads down the street in the direction of the university. As Shimada watches him go, he casually lights a cigarette. He calls over the soldier, talks quietly to him and hands him a piece of paper. The soldier salutes and heads off toward the embassy.

Lily steps away from the window, but her foot catches a curtain rail leaning against the wall and brings it crashing to the floor.

"Who's there?" Shimada asks, turning toward the window. "There are soldiers just around the corner. I need only raise my voice, and they will come running."

Lily peers out the window. Shimada is staring straight at her. There's a small pistol in his hand.

"It's me, Mr. Shimada."

"Stay there," he orders. He picks his way over the rubble and enters the house. Lily can hear his footsteps crunching over the debris on the floor as he works his way to the room she's in. She looks for another way out, but there is only the broken window, which is hemmed with long shards of glass. She pulls her jacket tightly around herself and watches the door.

When Shimada enters, he has a broad smile on his face. There's no sign of his pistol. "My dear Lily," he says. "This is such a pleasant surprise. What brings you here?"

"I was picking up supplies from the hospital."

"But you must have gone astray. This house is not on the route between the university and the hospital."

Shimada is slowly moving forward, and Lily calculates her chances of barging past him and making her escape. They're not good. He isn't tall, but he's stocky and probably strong enough to catch and hold her. Even if she got away, she would attract attention, running through the streets by the Japanese embassy. Guards would come from all directions.

"I took a detour to avoid a patrol."

Shimada nods. "And your detour took you to a bedroom"—his eyes drift over to the bed in the corner—"right beside the spot where I was having a conversation with your friend Neil Peterson?"

Lily stays silent.

"What did you hear of our conversation?"

"Just something about a visa."

"Hmmm." Shimada tilts his head. He blinks behind his thick glasses. "Dear Lily. I wish I could believe you."

"That's all I heard."

"Well, let us suppose for the moment that what you say is true. You must know that Peterson is leaving the day after tomorrow and wishes you to go with him."

"And you are helping him get a visa for me."

"Indeed. Even though acquiring one for you will be a difficult task."

"What if I don't want a visa?"

"You do not want to leave?" Shimada's eyes widen in surprise.

"Everyone wants to leave Nanjing, but for most people it is not possible. Peterson will leave here to go home. Nanjing *is* my home. I choose to stay." Only when the words leave her mouth does Lily realize they're true. Whatever Peterson does, she will stay.

Shimada stares at her for a long moment. "Life will be hard and dangerous here for some time. If you decide to stay, I can make it easier and safe for you." His eyes flick over her shoulder to the bed. "I might even be able to move you into the embassy."

"Thank you for your kind offer." Lily has to struggle to keep her voice even and her smile in place. What she wants to do is dig her fingernails deep into the fleshy cheeks of the pompous, leering face moving slowly closer. "I think I will take my chances at the university."

Shimada is so close that she can smell his sweat. He licks his lips eagerly and, without warning, raises his arms and shoves her hard in the chest. She staggers back two steps and falls on the bed. A cloud of plaster dust rises about her, and then Shimada is on top of her. He's surprisingly strong, and his weight is holding her immobile beneath him.

He's done this before, Lily thinks. She struggles, but to no avail. She tries to lift her head to bash Shimada in the face, but he easily avoids her effort and buries his head in her neck. She can feel his breath on her skin.

"This could have been much more pleasant," he says as he rubs himself against her. "But I will have you one way or another."

Lily twists her head and tries to bite his ear. She misses, but she catches a flap of skin on his neck and tastes blood.

Shimada yells in pain and raises himself up, twisting her right arm underneath her back. Something heavy in the right-hand pocket of his coat bumps against Lily's hip. "I will have you even if your arm is broken," he hisses. "You can accept your fate and then return to the university, or I can pass you on to the soldiers once I am finished. I would regret having to do that—you are very beautiful, and I fear you would not survive that experience—but I shall not hesitate to do so unless you cooperate."

Lily closes her eyes and breathes deeply. Her mind races. "You've won, Mr. Shimada. I won't struggle." She gives him what she hopes is a seductive smile and reaches for him, as if to pull him toward her. She slides her left hand into his coat pocket.

The gunshot is little more than a dull pop, muffled as it is by their bodies and his coat. Shimada's eyes widen. He lifts his head and tries to say something, but the small bullet that has traveled under his rib cage and torn through his lungs and heart before lodging itself in his left shoulder blade gives him no chance. He hiccups and makes a deep gurgling sound before his mouth fills with blood.

Lily heaves Shimada's body aside, slides off the bed and looks down to see his eyes blink one last time before they stare glassily at the ceiling. She closes her eyes and breathes deeply until her hands stop shaking.

She swallows, adjusts her clothing and carefully peers out the window. No one is moving on the street. There's no sign of the soldiers Shimada claimed were just around the corner. Lily walks around the bed and retrieves the pistol from Shimada's pocket. She peers at the body, shocked at what she has done. This person who just moments earlier was terrifying her and trying to rape her is now nothing more than a lump of flesh.

Lily hauls the corpse onto the floor and covers it with the blankets. If anyone glances in the window, all they will see is a wrecked room with a pile of bedclothes on the floor. It won't hide anything for long though. Sooner or later Shimada's disappearance will be noted, and the soldier will remember where his boss was last seen. The body will be discovered soon after that.

Lily takes another deep breath, then leaves the house and works her way through the gathering dark to the university.

CHAPTER FOURTEEN

Ashford, Ohio

Present Day

Tone woke up late to an empty house. He hadn't expected Theresa to be there, but Pike's absence was unusual. They had come back from the Blue Bar late, although not as drunk as on the previous occasion, and Pike usually slept until noon.

Tone showered and shaved. He made himself coffee and toast, then settled in front of his computer. The first email that caught his eye was from Seeger. It curtly summoned Tone to a meeting in the department boardroom at ten. The email was abrupt to the point of rudeness, and Seeger didn't even say what the meeting was about. Clearly Seeger was still pissed at his performance at the meeting, Tone thought.

He considered putting on his suit but decided against it. Soon enough, Seeger wouldn't be a part of his life and he wouldn't have to jump every time some dumb meeting was called.

Tone finished his coffee and looked out the window. The sun was shining, so he decided to walk to the university. He was feeling strangely calm. Things were going well. True, Theresa had decided to go back to China, but that was in some kind of weird effort to find herself. He didn't understand why she couldn't simply settle for success in America, but at least she wasn't dumping him for that asshole Quigley. In fact, it might work out well. He could leave all the baggage behind and enjoy a new, unencumbered start at MIT.

The thought of MIT brought a smile to Tone's lips. Working with some of the biggest names in the field would be awesome. "I'd like to thank the Nobel Committee," Tone said to himself, then laughed as he locked the front door behind him and set off down the tree-lined street.

An old man and his dog were tottering along the sidewalk toward him. Theresa had always taken the time to talk to the neighbors, complimenting the old lady next door on her flower garden and her husband on his vegetable patch. That sociability had earned them the occasional bunch of flowers and some delicious greenhouse tomatoes. But Tone had never had any time for pointless, idle chatter.

"Good morning," he said cheerily to the old man.

The man stopped in his tracks. "Good morning," he managed as Tone strode past. The dog gave a high-pitched yap and lunged at Tone's ankles, but its lead was too short.

As Tone walked, he found himself wondering if MIT had a drama department. He was surprised at how much he was enjoying being in Quigley's play. As soon as he'd realized Theresa was right when she told him acting was the ultimate in control, he had started looking at the whole thing differently. Hill had become a part of him—a part he could express without any fear of contradiction and that he could change how and when he wanted. In a way Hill was Tone's alter ego. He was impulsive and passionate—the two things Tone never allowed himself to be in real life.

Tone had practiced his lines relentlessly, and with that his stage fright had vanished. His acting was still not polished, but his growing relationship with the fictional Hill allowed him to bring an authenticity to the role that the audience could relate to. In fact, even before Pike had pointed him toward the communist soldier's book, it was this relationship with Hill that had made Tone think Quigley was wrong in making him the villain of the piece. Certainly it was in character for Hill to do something impetuous and dangerous, but he was a patriot and would never have stooped to betraying anyone to the Japanese, especially when it would have put Lily, whom he loved, in danger.

Tone was still pondering whether he could bring something to that evening's performance to suggest this when he entered the university campus. Quigley would be pissed, but Tone didn't care about that. He turned toward the physics building, then glanced over at the theater. He stopped.

This was symbolic. Physics and drama. Tone and Hill. Did they fit together, two sides of the same coin?

He was about to turn back when he noticed two figures. It took him a moment to recognize Theresa and Quigley. They were laughing at some shared joke and had stopped to hug each other. The hug morphed into a kiss that was much more than a friendly goodbye. Then, arm in arm, they disappeared through the door into the theater.

Tone's sense of calm evaporated to be replaced by anger. The hug had been too long and the kiss too intimate for mere friends, and where had they come from?

Tone stormed into the physics building and stomped along the corridor toward the boardroom. His fists were clenched and he was breathing heavily.

Two students walking the other way looked at him oddly and gave him a wide berth. Tone ignored them. Seeger had better have a good reason for calling this meeting.

He turned a corner and almost collided with Pike. His friend was slouching along with his head down. "Pike! What're you doing here?"

Pike snapped his head up and stared at Tone. His eyes were wide with fear. The image of a fat, scared rabbit flashed unkindly through Tone's head.

"What's the matter?"

Pike shook his head and mumbled something that sounded like "Sorry." He pushed past Tone and broke into a stumbling run down the corridor.

Tone stared after him. What the hell was going on? He continued down the corridor and pushed his way into the boardroom. His anger was now intertwined with worry and confusion.

Seeger sat at the center of a long table, flanked by four other members of staff. "Ah, Mr. Zhang, come in." He gestured to a chair facing the table. "Take a seat." As Tone sat, Seeger added, "I'm sure you know Professors Thompson, Spry, Faulkner and McKenzie." The four glared stonily at Tone as Seeger spoke. "Together we constitute the ad hoc ethics committee, and we are here today to get to the bottom of a very serious matter."

Tone could think of nothing to say, so he simply nodded.

Seeger held up a sheaf of papers in his right hand. "This is an essay you submitted as a requirement for Physics 422. If you recall, it was an upper-level course that I taught on advanced optics."

"I took it because of the difficulties involved in observing the results of low-temperature experiments," Tone said in a monotone. "As I recall, you gave me an A for this paper and in the course overall."

"Indeed I did. You undertook some fine work as a part of that course."

Seeger paused, a smirk on his face. Tone pushed away the urge to leap across the table and knock the smirk down his throat.

"Your friend Pike Zhou has not undertaken stellar work in this course. And yet"—Seeger lifted a second sheaf of papers—"he has managed to produce a piece of work remarkably similar to your own."

He and the other committee members sat in silence while the implications of what he'd said sank in. Tone was stunned. Yes, he'd let Pike see the paper to get some ideas for his own, but he'd done that dozens of times before. Maybe Pike had gotten lazy and relied too heavily on Tone's ideas. Maybe Seeger was making a mountain out of a molehill because he was still annoyed with Tone.

"Can I see the papers?"

"By all means." Seeger slid the two essays across the desk.

The instant Tone glanced from one to the other, a sickening void opened in his gut. The two were almost identical, word for word. This was no molehill.

The mask he had so carefully constructed crumbled, and Tone was suddenly a small, scared boy who had been caught doing something naughty by his elders—or, even worse, cornered by the school bully. He felt like weeping.

"I don't understand," he mumbled.

"It's quite simple," Seeger said. He spoke slowly, as if to savor the moment. "This is as straightforward a case of plagiarism as I have seen in twenty years of teaching."

"I didn't know Pike was going to copy it," Tone whined weakly.

"So you admit giving him your old paper?"

"Yes." Tone was having trouble forcing the words out. "But just to give him ideas. I never intended for him to copy it."

"Nevertheless, he did. And this is not the first time this has happened, is it?"

"What?" Tone looked up.

The other committee members refused to meet his eye, but Seeger stared straight at him.

"When this case of cheating came to light, we went back through Pike Zhou's previous submissions and compared them to papers you submitted in earlier years. While none were as blatantly copied as this one, we found far too many similarities for them to be coincidence. The plagiarism is extensive and has been going on for a considerable time. In fact, I would go so far as to say that Mr. Zhou could not have maintained a grade sufficient to keep him at this institution without your assistance."

"I only wanted to help him."

"And in doing so, you stepped well over the bounds of what is academically acceptable in a research institute that wishes to maintain reputability within the scientific community."

Seeger kept talking, but Tone barely listened. He was struggling to regain control of his inner turmoil and anger. Pike had been too lazy or too drunk to bother reworking the papers enough to hide the connection? How could he possibly have thought he would get away with it? For God's sake, they *both* had Seeger as professor of this course! He couldn't help but notice! This was what you got for trying to help people. He was going to beat the shit out of Pike when he caught him.

Seeger's voice had risen enough to intrude into Tone's thoughts.

"I asked you if you know what the consequences of plagiarism are."

"Dismissal from the faculty," Tone mumbled. "Pike will have to be dismissed."

"That has already been done," Seeger said.

Tone had a momentary flash of pity for Pike, who would have to go back to China—and his father—in disgrace, but Seeger was still talking. "I was asking if you know what the consequences are for *you*."

"For me?" Tone asked. "I didn't plagiarize anything."

"Plagiarism is a two-way street, and in this case it has been going on for a long time. As a university with a reputation to maintain, we cannot be seen to be producing graduates who cannot meet the basic requirements without cheating."

"Fine," Tone said, focusing his anger on Seeger's pomposity. "So you've dismissed Pike and solved that problem. You can't dismiss me. My PhD is complete and awarded. Besides, none of this has anything to do with my research. As you are well aware, it is original and of the highest quality. Quite frankly, I doubt if there is anyone at this precious university of yours who is capable of adding anything to my work."

The undisguised hatred in Seeger's expression made Tone wonder if he had gone too far, but he hadn't said anything that wasn't true.

"You are correct in saying we cannot dismiss you, Mr. Zhang." Seeger's voice was flat. "However, the committee members and I, after lengthy deliberations, have decided that we cannot simply let the matter slide. If word were to get out that you were part of a scheme to allow an incompetent student to be awarded a fraudulent degree—or if you repeated this nonsense elsewhere and we were seen to have done nothing to prevent it—it would reflect very badly on Eastern University."

Tone's mind whirled with the possibilities he could be facing. Before he could settle on one, Seeger smiled coldly and continued.

"We have decided that the correct course of action is for us to craft a document outlining in the fullest detail this sordid affair and your involvement in it and then submit that document to the Kelvin Fellowship board at MIT."

It took a long moment for Seeger's words to sink in. Then Tone fell apart.

"You can't!" he cried.

"We can, and we shall. This is the unanimous decision of the ethics committee. The letter, with the appropriate supporting documentation, will be sent out tomorrow."

Tone stared at each of the committee members in turn. He saw no sympathy in anyone's eyes, although Spry and McKenzie looked distinctly uncomfortable.

"MIT will withdraw the Kelvin Fellowship," he sputtered.

"In all probability they will," Seeger said. "It's certainly what I would do under the circumstances."

Tone sat frozen for a long moment as his anger returned. Then, without warning, he lunged across the table, sending papers, pens and books scattering to the floor. He grabbed for Seeger's lapels, but the table was too broad and the man was too quick, pushing himself back as the other committee members scrambled to the sides.

"You slimy, pretentious prick!" Tone screamed. "I'll kill you! You understand *nothing*! You've never had a creative thought or written a worthwhile word in your entire miserable career! You're not fit to read the *abstract* of one of my papers, let alone stand in the way of what I intend to achieve!"

Tone slumped across the table. Faulkner was on his cell to campus security. No one said a word as Tone's violent anger turned to self-pity. Deep inside he knew his bluster was pointless. Perhaps he could get a teaching post at a small college, but his chance of doing high-level research at any of the few universities that had enough funding and facilities to support the kind of work he wanted to do had vanished. Seeger would see to that. His life was in ruins.

Tears streamed down Tone's cheeks as he pushed himself off the table and stumbled toward the door. He barged past the security guard who was answering Faulkner's call and headed down the corridor.

Barely aware of where he was going, Tone staggered home. His mind was a mess of conflicting thoughts, and his emotions seesawed between rage and self-indulgent misery. The rage had him swearing violently under his breath, kicking anything in his way and concocting ever-more brutal ways of exacting revenge on those who had destroyed his life in the space of a few hours. The misery wracked his body with choking sobs that soaked the front of his shirt with tears. He pictured hurling himself in front of a truck or leaping from a high bridge.

By the time he finally stumbled up the front steps of the house, he was exhausted. He half expected Pike to be sitting on the couch, killing aliens, but the house was empty. Tone threw himself onto his bed and buried his face in the pillow.

Gradually his mind calmed and his emotions stabilized. He still felt angry and miserable, but he had regained control. He could think rationally to some degree. He replayed the morning in his head, focusing on the people responsible for his destruction.

Seeing Theresa kiss Quigley had been a blow, but oddly he felt little animosity toward her. Sure, she had betrayed him, but he'd already begun to say goodbye when she told him she wasn't coming to MIT with him. Allen Quigley was the one he felt hostile toward. He'd probably given Tone the role of Hill in hopes that he would embarrass himself horribly onstage. And he'd cast Theresa as his lover so he could seduce her. He had succeeded, and Tone couldn't forgive him for that.

Then there was that pompous loser Seeger and his gutless ethics committee. Seeger could have ignored Pike's stupidity and allowed Tone to go on and achieve great things, but no, he had to bring him down. He had probably been jealous of Tone's talent all along and couldn't resist taking advantage when the opportunity presented itself.

But what about Pike and his role in this? His thoughtless idiocy had triggered the worst moment in Tone's life. And yet...Tone couldn't hate him. Pike had done nothing vindictive or out of character, and Tone had given him his old assignments of his own free will. Tone's arrogant assumption that no one would spot anything was as much to blame as Pike's stupidity.

No, Tone felt no anger at either Theresa or Pike. They, like him, were just struggling in their own ways to survive and be successful in an alien culture. It was Quigley and Seeger who deserved to suffer. They were the ones who manipulated the people around them for their own gratification, who made self-seeking decisions and expected the world to fall into line with them. They were the mean, opportunistic slimeballs who had ruined Tone's life, destroyed Pike's chance to stay wealthy and keep his father proud of him, and exploited and used Theresa.

Tone hauled himself up to sit against the pillows. He felt unnaturally calm, but he was restless. He needed something to do. He reached over and pulled the revolver out of the bedside table. Slowly and methodically he dismantled the gun the way Pike had shown him. Using his bedsheets, and not caring about the oil and grease stains he was putting on them, he cleaned every part meticulously. Then he took the small bottle of gun oil that had come with the weapon and oiled everything. When he was done he dropped the bottle, oblivious to it emptying out on the duvet. Efficiently he put the revolver back together and spun the chamber.

"Shit, man. You're not going to do anything stupid, are you?"

Tone looked up to see Pike standing in the bedroom doorway. He looked pitiful, and Tone had to suppress an urge to laugh.

"No," he said, dropping the gun onto his lap. "You've done something stupid enough for both of us."

"Sorry. Sorry. Sorry."

Pike looked so sad that this time Tone couldn't stop the laugh.

"What's so funny?" Pike asked, a puzzled look pushing the misery off his face.

"You are," Tone said once he'd quit laughing. "You're a hopeless lump of lard who's made staggeringly stupid decisions, but what's done is done. The person to blame is Seeger. It must have been obvious to him from the beginning that you were hopeless at physics. He let you in because you were a warm body paying high international student fees. He was probably as happy as you that you were scraping through and would be paying for another semester. He didn't give a shit about you until you screwed up so badly he couldn't ignore it anymore."

"What about you? Seeger didn't take you on just for the money."

"Prestige. He was smart enough to know that I was doing groundbreaking work. He figured he could ride my coattails and make himself and his department look good. But as soon as I threatened to become a liability, I got dumped."

"At least you've still got MIT to go to."

Tone shook his head. "Seeger and his stupid committee are sending a report to the Kelvin Fellowship board. They'll withdraw the funding. MIT won't touch me with a ten-foot pole now—and probably neither will any other high-level research facility."

The look of unspeakable sadness on Tone's face ripped at Pike's guts. "I'm *so* sorry, man."

"Like I said, it's not entirely your fault. You're as screwed by this mess as I am. I don't blame you."

"What will you do?"

"I don't know." Tone forced a wry smile. "A few weeks ago I had everything—a fast track to fame and fortune, and a beautiful girl." He laughed bitterly. "Now Seeger's destroyed the first, and Quigley's taken the second."

"You don't know that."

Tone fiddled distractedly with the revolver. "I saw them outside the theater. He was all over her. They were almost screwing in public."

Pike's gaze drifted to the revolver on Tone's lap. "You're not going to do anything crazy, are you?"

Tone hesitated for so long it made Pike nervous. But then he swallowed hard and dropped the gun into the bedside drawer. "What are *you* going to do? Your dad will have a fit. He won't keep sending you money now."

"Yeah," Pike agreed. "The thing I've feared most for the last four years has finally happened—I've screwed up one too many times." He came into the room and sat on the end of

Tone's bed. "I've done a lot of thinking over the past couple of hours. Once I got over the shock, I realized that part of me is relieved. It's like I've been cut free. Dad'll be seriously pissed, and I'll never see another dollar from him, but I can do what I want. And one thing I'll say for the old man is that he was generous. Even I couldn't spend it all, so I've managed to save up a fair bit—enough for a few months, at least. And if I keep quiet, maybe I can bank another couple of payments before he gets suspicious. Come summer, I'll take that road trip out west. I should get a good dollar for the car on the coast, and then I'll find a decent little school with a good program in Asian studies."

"The American dream!" Tone said.

Pike missed the sarcasm in his voice and said, "Half of it anyway. I guess I'll see the other half as well—flipping burgers in a greasy spoon to pay the rent. But what the hell? I'll get by."

Tone swung his legs off the bed and stood up. He took Pike's hand and pulled him to his feet.

"I'm proud of you, man. You're flexible. I tried to change the world to suit me. Now I've got nothing left. But you, you're the ultimate survivor." He drew Pike into a hug. "I wish you all the best. I really do."

Surprised by the display of emotion, Pike still managed to return the hug. "And back at you, man. It'll all work out. You'll see."

Tone let go. "Now bugger off and play your video game. I've got to get ready for the play."

"You're still going through with that?"

"It's all I've got left." He shrugged. "And we all need a swan song. Will you come and witness mine?"

Something in Tone's voice made Pike hesitate, but he said, "Of course, man. I'll be there. Wouldn't miss it."

CHAPTER FIFTEEN

Nanjing, Jiangsu

Morning, December 15, 1937

In that moment between sleep and wakefulness, Lily basks in a warm glow of happiness. Then the past and the present rush in to hurl her into a new day. She reaches under her pillow until her fingers touch the cold, confirming metal of Shimada's pistol. It's all real. Last night she killed someone.

She had carefully avoided Peterson and Hill when she got back to the university, not certain she could hold it together if she saw them. Only when she was safely back in her room did she collapse fully clothed on her bed and weep. She'd wept until exhaustion overcame her and she fell into a fitful sleep. Now she has to get up and face another day. More than that, she has to face the first day in a changed world. Now she's a murderer.

Lily rolls off her bed, undresses and washes herself as well as she can in the basin of cold water in the corner. She scrubs until her skin is raw, trying to rub Shimada off her. It doesn't work. He'll be with her forever.

Shivering with cold, she dresses. She manages two steps toward the door before she freezes. She should stay here. Her room is safe. She's alone. She doesn't have to talk to anyone. But she *wants* to talk to someone. The burden of last night is unbearably heavy, and she has to share it. But with whom? She sits on the edge of the bed. She can't trust Neil anymore. What did he offer Shimada in exchange for the visa? She trusts Hill, but he has enough weight of his own to carry with Chen. Still...

Lily is jerked to her feet by a loud knock on her door. She grabs the pistol. Her first thought is that Japanese soldiers have come to execute her for killing Shimada. She's hugely relieved to hear Hill's voice.

"Are you in there?" he calls. "It's late, and Peterson's going crazy worrying about the performance this afternoon."

His arrival's a sign, Lily thinks. She throws the door open and flings herself into his arms, almost knocking him off his feet.

"What?" is all he can manage before she drags him into her room and closes the door.

"I'm so happy to see you," she says, pulling the startled Hill over to sit on the edge of the bed. "I was thinking about you. Something terrible has happened."

"Calm down." Hill puts an arm around Lily's shoulders. "What's happened? And put that gun down before it goes off."

Lily drops the gun on the bed. "On the way back from the hospital yesterday, I saw Neil." Now that she's begun, there's no stopping her, and the whole story comes out in a rush. Hill listens in astonished silence.

When she finishes, he pulls her into a hug and strokes her hair. "You were so brave," he says.

Lily feels on the verge of tears, but she fights them and pulls away from him. "I killed a man, Hill."

"A man who deserved to die. Shimada was no better than Masao or the soldiers manning the machine guns down by the river. You are incredibly brave. You did the right thing. You fought for your honor and killed the man who tried to take it. You have done one shining thing in the midst of all this darkness. I wish I had been there. I would have helped you kill him."

"Thank you, Hill." Lily gently touches his cheek. "But Shimada was going to take you to study theater in Kyoto."

"That was in a different world. When Shimada first mentioned the idea in Shanghai, I saw it as a way to escape, as Chen had done. But after what you and I have seen here…" He trails off, shaking his head.

"What will we do? I'm almost certain that Neil has betrayed Chen and the others to the Japanese in exchange for a visa for me."

"It doesn't matter. Shimada can't tell anyone now."

"I don't know. There was a soldier there. Shimada spoke to him and gave him a note of some kind. The soldier left before Shimada found me. He might have been taking a message to Masao."

"It still doesn't matter," he says. "Chen left during the night."

"Chen's left the Safety Zone?"

"He took the most seriously wounded of his men to the hospital, then he and the fittest left before dawn. They'll split up and hide until tonight and then try to escape from the city. Before he left, Chen and I had a long talk. He told me all the things he had done in the years he was away. He said he has lost faith in our army. The soldiers are brave, but they are badly trained and led, and the officers and politicians are corrupt. Supplies that should go to the troops are stolen. Money that should buy us better guns, tanks and planes instead lines the pockets of people who have never even seen a Japanese soldier."

"So it's hopeless?" Lily asks. "We cannot win this war?"

"Not on our own. Maybe one day the Americans will help us. Until then there is only one army fighting the Japanese properly, and that is the Red Army."

"The communists?"

Hill nods. "That's where Chen's going—north to join the Red Army."

"What will you do?"

"I will join him. We've arranged to meet on the road to Wuhan in one week."

"I'll come with you." It's a statement, not a question. "And I have a gun." Lily picks up the pistol, shoves it into her jacket pocket and stands up.

Hill grabs her hands. "You can't, Lily. It's too dangerous. It will be like going on the Long March."

"You said I was incredibly brave."

"You are."

"And didn't women go on the Long March?"

"They did."

"Then I am going with you. Besides, traveling with a woman will be less suspicious, and I can't stay here. Shimada's body will soon be found. Masao will stop at nothing to find out who killed him. Peterson is going back to America, and you are going on a long march. Would you like me to be the one who stays behind and faces Masao's wrath?"

"Of course not." Hill shakes his head and sighs. "I should know better than to try to stop you from doing anything. But first, my beautiful, brave Lily, we must survive today."

CHAPTER SIXTEEN

Ashford, Ohio

Present Day

Tone closed the bedroom door and stared, unblinking, at the bedside table. His jaw was clenched, and the tendons in his neck stood out like strands of taut wire. He was breathing heavily. When he'd relaxed, he stripped off his clothes and stood under the shower for a long time. Then he dried himself, dressed in sweatpants and a T-shirt, packed his backpack and snuck out of the house without disturbing Pike.

He took a long, rambling walk around Ashford, finally arriving at the Blue Bar. He took a stool and placed his backpack on the one beside him. The place was deserted except for a young Chinese couple deep in conversation in a corner booth. The barman looked intensely bored as he rearranged bottles and stacked clean glasses. Tone ordered two drinks—one from the blue bottle at the extreme left of the line, the other from the one at the extreme right. The barman looked at him oddly but poured without comment. Tone paid and the man went back to his chores.

"Here's to you, Pike," Tone said, lifting his glass in salute to the row of bottles. He downed the first drink. It tasted sickly sweet.

"What'd you say?" the barman asked.

"Nothing."

The barman shrugged and went back to ignoring him.

"And here's to you, Theresa." He lifted the shot glass to his own reflection in the mirror behind the bar and drank. It tasted no better than the first drink.

Tone placed the empty glass on the bar, lifted his backpack and stood. He took a couple of steps toward the door, then turned and walked over to the couple in the corner. They were leaning across the table, holding hands, and so engrossed with each other that they didn't notice him until he was standing over them. "Don't ever forget who you are," he said to their surprised faces. Before they could respond, he walked out of the bar.

At the university campus he walked to the middle of the main quadrangle. He stared long and hard at the physics building and the theater in turn. Then he entered the physics building and walked the entire length of the main corridor. He met no one he knew, although a couple of undergraduates nodded to him. He hesitated by the door of the lab where he had done most of his research, but he didn't enter.

After Tone left the physics building, he headed for the Neil Peterson Theater. He stood at the auditorium door for a moment, listening to the sounds of Quigley's final rehearsal. It was late afternoon, but the day was still hot and humid. After his long walk and two drinks on an empty stomach, Tone was feeling slightly light-headed. He walked over to the cafeteria. The dining hall was noisy with students talking and laughing. A few even appeared to be trying to work.

Tone bought himself a coffee and a bacon sandwich and sat at a table in the corner. As he ate, he looked around. Almost half the students were Chinese. Clustered in small groups, most were speaking Mandarin, although Tone caught Cantonese and snippets of Wu and Hakka. He smiled slightly. The English speakers in the room probably thought all the Chinese were speaking the same language, yet Hakka was as different from Mandarin as French was from Spanish.

It's like a room in the Tower of Babel, Tone thought. What were they all discussing, arguing about or laughing at? Probably nothing. It was just empty noise. He marveled at how shallow everyone was.

He finished his sandwich and took his laptop out of his backpack. As he sipped his coffee, he composed a long email. He deleted several versions and edited extensively between long periods of contemplation in which he was barely aware of his surroundings. When he was satisfied with the text, he set up a delayed delivery and closed his computer. He drained the last of his cold coffee and carefully placed his paper cup and plate in the recycling. It was already dusk by the time he left and headed over to the theater.

"Tone! Where the hell have you been? You missed the entire afternoon rehearsal." Quigley was standing at the center of the stage with Theresa beside him. A few costumed cast members and some backstage crew were milling around them, making last-minute adjustments to the set. Everyone stopped what they were doing and stared at Tone, who ignored the attention and climbed onto the stage.

Theresa moved to intercept him as Quigley kept talking. "The curtain goes up in an hour, and there are script changes to learn. This is seriously unprofessional. You're putting the entire project in jeopardy."

Tone simply smiled at Quigley and headed backstage. Theresa fell into step beside him. She was already in costume—a form-fitting cheongsam dress, high at the neck and sleeveless. It was slit on one side from ankle to thigh. Her hair was pulled back in a tight bun, and subtle makeup highlighted her full lips and piercing eyes. Tone almost cried at her beauty.

"Allen's been like this all day," she said. "He's totally stressed. Don't worry about the script changes. They're minor, and no one will care if you use them or not." Outside the dressing room she placed a hand on Tone's arm, stopping him. "Where *have* you been? Are you okay? Pike called and told me what happened with Seeger this morning."

"I'm okay," Tone muttered, pushing into the crowded dressing room. He fought his way over to where his costume hung and changed into it. Then he found space at a mirror and started putting on his makeup.

As he was applying the finishing touches, Quigley came in. He pointedly ignored Tone.

"Everyone ready?" he asked. A murmur of assent ran through the room. "Excellent. The audience is coming in. Looks like it'll be a full house. You were all awesome last night, and we polished a few rough edges this afternoon"—Quigley flashed Tone a look—"so it'll be brilliant this evening. Positions in five minutes. Break a leg."

The actors hustled to finish their preparations or simply fiddled with their costumes to distract themselves. Then they began to drift out to take their places onstage or behind the curtains. Tone was one of the last to leave. At the stage, he peered through a slit in the curtains and examined the audience. Quigley was right—it was a full house. Most of those in the audience were Chinese students, but there were also several faculty members, including Seeger, who sat in the front row, alongside the reporter from the local paper.

Tone searched for Pike and was disappointed not to see him. But just as the lights dimmed, he saw his friend slip in the back door, look around in vain for an empty seat and take up a position against the wall. With a smile Tone took his own place at the edge of the stage, ready for his entrance.

Quigley and Theresa stood center stage. She looked over at Tone questioningly. He composed his face into an expressionless mask and nodded slightly. She smiled.

Quigley whispered something to Theresa and slipped through the curtains. The buzz in the audience disappeared, and Tone heard Quigley give the same introduction as he had the night before. When he was done Quigley slipped back through the curtains, followed by polite applause. The curtains parted, and a photograph of the burning Nanjing skyline was projected onto the screen at the back of the stage.

As the play progressed, the audience became more and more drawn into Quigley's tale of what might have happened to the famous playwright in China so many years earlier. The confidence of the actors grew with each scene, until they and the audience members believed they'd been transported to a makeshift theater stage in the Safety Zone of war-torn Nanjing in the midst of a horrific massacre. The projected images of exploding bombs, marching soldiers and frightened refugees added authenticity to the proceedings. Simple drumming provided the soundtrack, drawing the audience toward the climax of the play.

The performance of Guan Hanqing's play *Lord Guan Goes to the Feast* had just been completed before an audience of Japanese officers and a few foreign missionaries and businessmen. Quigley, Theresa and Tone—in their roles as Peterson, Lily and Hill—stood in the middle of the stage, surrounded by actors playing wounded Chinese soldiers dressed in the thirteenth-century costumes of Guan Hanqing's play. A Japanese general, accompanied by Shimada and followed by several armed soldiers, burst onto the stage from the wings. The soldiers surrounded the wounded Chinese.

One attempted to break away and was shot. Theresa/Lily screamed. Tone/Hill turned away and knelt over the shot boy.

Theresa/Lily: What is going on? These are refugees playing the roles of wounded soldiers. We had an agreement. Neil, make them stop. Tell them they can't do this. We had an agreement.

Allen/Peterson: General, we spoke about this only a few days ago. You agreed to let us put on the play. Now you invade us and shoot one of our actors? I demand that you remove your soldiers immediately.

Shimada: I am sorry, Neil, but that will not be possible. The general is doing what he has to. These men are soldiers of an enemy army, and we are at war.

Theresa/Lily: They're not soldiers—they're boys. Helpless, harmless boys. The one you shot was only fifteen years old. They are actors playing roles.

Shimada: That is not the information we have. All of you "actors," remove your bandages. Do it! Or you will be shot just as your companion was!

Allen/Peterson: This is preposterous.

Shimada: Preposterous, is it? I must say that I admire your dedication to your art—actually wounding your actors so that they can live and feel the roles you have given them. Some wounds even seem to have been inflicted several days ago. See? That one is partly healed, and, oh dear, this one seems to be infected.

The General: Take them away. We know how to deal with the enemy.

Theresa/Lily: I beg you. Where is your humanity?

Allen/Peterson: They have no humanity. But Shimada, how did you know? This was obviously planned in advance. The soldiers were just waiting for the order to move in.

Shimada: The general has a very good information network. Nothing can happen without him finding out.

Allen/Peterson: But we were careful. Very few people knew. We must have been betrayed by someone... [He looks around the stage and his eyes rest on Hill.] Hill, it was you! I often wondered how you, a Chinese man of military age, could move about so easily. You made a deal with Shimada, and he told the general. You betrayed these boys to save your own miserable life. What did Shimada offer you? The lives of your family? The chance to study in Japan? To be like a pet, trotted out whenever the Japanese want to show how generous they are to their conquered subjects? Do you have an answer?

Theresa/Lily: Hill, can what Neil says be true?

Allen/Peterson: He cannot say anything. He has no answer. Hill betrayed us both.

Tone sneaked off the stage after the general, Shimada, the soldiers and their prisoners. The lights dimmed on Allen and Theresa. Old black-and-white pictures of ruined buildings, terrified women and children, and triumphant Japanese soldiers standing beside piles of bodies flickered across the screen. Eventually the image of a gunboat on the Yangtze River settled in place. The lights went up and revealed the stage, empty but for Allen and Theresa, dressed in civilian clothes.

Allen/Peterson: I think the worst is over now.

Theresa/Lily: The worst in Nanjing, maybe. But the killing and the dying will go on for many years all across China, and perhaps all across the world.

Allen/Peterson: Not for us. That's an American gunboat out on the river. I spoke with the captain down at the docks. He's heading downriver tomorrow. He told me there's a liner at Shanghai leaving for San Francisco at the end of the week. He's prepared to take us with him, and he thinks we'll be able to transfer to the liner. Then we'll be on our way. It'll be hell to organize, but once we're on board, they won't be able to stop us. We can worry about the paperwork once we're safe in San Francisco. This is our chance. We can escape. We can go home.

Theresa/Lily: It's your home, Neil, not mine.

Allen /Peterson: What do you mean? You'll be welcome there. It can be your home too.

Theresa/Lily: I'm not coming with you.

Allen/Peterson: Why? You have to come with me. We have to tell the story of what we have seen here—the courage and bravery in the face of such unbelievable horror. The world must know.

Theresa/Lily: I agree the world must know, but that is your job. You're the storyteller, and you're the American. You can make your people understand. I would just be an exotic stranger by your side. My people are still here, suffering, dying, surviving. I can't leave them. I would feel like a coward running away.

Allen/Peterson: But you're just one person. What difference can you make?

Theresa/Lily: I make a difference with every bandage I tie, with every boy I save from the Japanese, with every square of canvas I find for a roof for a homeless family, and with every drop of milk I give to a starving baby. You go and tell your story, Neil. Tell our *story. Make people understand. Change the world. But I have to stay.*

Allen/Peterson: But I love you, Lily.

Theresa/Lily: And I love you, Neil. But what's love worth in this hellish place we've all created here? The forces being unleashed on the world will overwhelm mere love. Hill loved me just as you do, and yet he betrayed us all.

The pair embraced, and the lights went up to thunderous applause. Quigley and Theresa bowed. Quigley beckoned everyone else onstage. The audience stood, stamped, applauded and whistled even harder. All the principals took individual bows. Everyone grinned from ear to ear—everyone except Tone, who stood stone-faced and barely bent into his bow.

"Thank you," Quigley said as the applause died away, "on behalf of all of us, and especially on behalf of Neil Peterson. We have told his story. Thank you for listening." He took Theresa's hand, bowed one last time and began to lead the cast away.

At that moment Tone stepped to the front of the stage and addressed the audience. "Thank you all for coming to watch our show," he said in a loud, clear voice.

Quigley, Theresa and the other actors stopped and turned to look at him. Audience members halted in the midst of collecting their bags and putting on their jackets. There were many puzzled faces. Quigley's expression was tinged with anger.

"I too would like to thank Neil Peterson for giving us so much to think about," Tone went on, not caring about the confusion he was creating. "Tonight you have been privileged to share one man's interpretation of the great mystery of Peterson's life. It was powerfully and movingly done." There was a short burst of applause. "But it is only one man's interpretation. Personally, I do not believe that Hill Chao betrayed the soldiers in the Safety Zone. It was not in his character, and he went on to fight long and hard for the People's Liberation Army against the Japanese. No, I believe it was Peterson himself who betrayed the wounded soldiers in his care."

A murmur ran through the audience. Quigley took a step forward, but Theresa held him back.

"This interpretation explains many things—not least Peterson's reluctance to complete his *magnum opus*. What I find fascinating about him is his decision-making. Very few of the decisions we make every day are absolute—most lead only to other decisions, and those later decisions can often reverse the earlier ones. Peterson decided to go to China, and then he decided to stay in Nanjing with Lily when the foreign diplomats left. Later he decided to leave both Nanjing and China and resume his life in America. On the surface, he reversed his earlier decisions, but underneath was the decision he could never reverse—his betrayal of the wounded soldiers. That decision came very close to destroying him."

Quigley pulled free of Theresa and stepped toward Tone. "What is the point of all of this?" he demanded.

When Tone turned, Quigley saw something in his face that stopped him in his tracks.

"The point, Allen," he spat, "is that sometimes we make decisions we cannot reverse and cannot live with. Sometimes we thoughtlessly make decisions that others cannot reverse or live with."

In one smooth movement Tone drew the revolver out of the folds of his costume and pointed it at Quigley's head. An audible gasp ran through the onlookers, and then the room went dead quiet.

"You decided to cast me in the role of Hill so I would make a fool of myself onstage and also be the villain of your play. You decided to do this in order to take Theresa from me."

Theresa opened her mouth to say something, but a hard stare from Tone stopped her.

"Is that true?" he asked Quigley.

Quigley's mouth was working, but no sound was coming out. He looked deathly pale even with heavy makeup on, and his hands were shaking visibly. He nodded.

"What is even worse, you wrote this play for selfish reasons. You wanted Peterson to be a hero so you could ride higher on the great man's coattails. He had to be perfect. You deliberately ignored any information that conflicted with your precious theory that Hill was the traitor."

"I didn't," Quigley whined.

Tone stepped forward until the muzzle of the revolver was inches from Quigley's forehead. He could see the beads of sweat breaking through the makeup.

"You did. When Pike showed me the journal that mentioned Hill Chao fighting with Mao's army, I noticed you were the last person to sign it out. At the very least, that journal cast significant doubt on Hill's guilt, and you yourself told me that it changed the interpretation. Yet you ignored the evidence. You didn't want your precious American playwright to be tainted, so you framed the Chinese character. Is that true?"

Quigley swallowed hard and whispered, "Yes."

"You're an actor," Tone said. "Project your voice."

"Yes!" Quigley said, loudly enough for the entire theater to hear.

Tone smiled and pulled the trigger.

The click of the hammer coming down on the empty chamber was deafening in the tense silence. Quigley's knees buckled, and he sagged to the stage, sobbing.

Theresa moved in front of Quigley's collapsed form before Tone could fire again. She looked up at him. "Stop it," she pleaded.

His smile broadened. "It's about to stop," he said. "I wish you good luck back in China."

"Come with me," she said.

Tone shook his head and moved to the edge of the stage. With slow deliberation he pointed the revolver at Seeger, who was standing in the front row, frozen with the other stunned audience members.

"You made decisions as well, Professor Seeger."

"I-I-I only had the good of the department and the university in my mind," Seeger stammered.

Tone laughed—a harsh, mirthless sound. "You only had your own good in that petty little mind of yours. You made the decision to bring me here because it would look good on you to have someone doing original work in your department. But you were always jealous. I made a mistake, and you used it to destroy me. To make it impossible for me to do what I was destined to do—reach the heights to which you could never aspire."

"That's not—I—"

"Shut up," Tone ordered softly. "All I say is true, isn't it?"

Seeger hesitated and then nodded faintly. Tone squeezed the trigger, and another click echoed around the hall.

While Tone was humiliating Seeger, Pike had been moving slowly down the side aisle. Now Tone turned to him.

"No, Pike, my friend." He waved the gun in his general direction. "This is not something that can be solved by a night in the Blue Bar. Go and enjoy your freedom."

"Don't do it," Pike said. He was scared, but he kept moving forward. For a long moment Tone steadied the gun so that it pointed directly at him. Pike forced himself to take another step.

Tone winked at Pike and turned back to the audience. "It's always about decisions," he said. "We make a choice, then another and another. Eventually we end up somewhere we couldn't even have imagined when we made the first choice.

If we're lucky, we can go back and reverse some choices, but we can never go back all the way. Our choices change us and those around us." Tone's smile was gone now. His face was expressionless as he raised the revolver to his temple. "There's really only one decision—one choice—that never allows another."

"Nooooooo!" Pike yelled. It was a clear, sharp sound in the superb acoustics of the Neil Peterson Theater, but the end of it was cut off by the deafening gunshot.

CHAPTER SEVENTEEN

Nanjing, Jiangsu

Afternoon, December 15, 1937

"Where the hell is everybody?" Peterson is standing in the center of the nearly empty stage. Only a few of the cast members of *Lord Guan Goes to the Feast* are hovering in the background, watching him. "We have a major production beginning in a couple of hours, and we have no extras. And where are Lily and Hill?"

"Here," Hill says as he and Lily come in the theater door. They walk down the aisle and up onto the stage.

"Where were you last night?" Peterson asks Lily.

"I went out for a walk."

He looks confused. "You went for a walk? In the middle of a fucking battle, you went for a walk? Are you insane? This isn't Central Park. You could have been killed."

"I know it's not Central Park, Neil. It's my city, and as you can see, I wasn't killed."

Lily's soft voice seems to calm Peterson's anger. He shakes his head. "I'm sorry, but things are falling apart." He looks at Hill. "Where are the extras?"

"Chen and his men left last night."

"Left?! What do you mean?"

"Exactly that," Hill says, matching Lily's calm. "They are no longer here. They won't be in your play."

"They have to be. We need soldiers in the background."

"We have a couple of hours," Hill says. "The extras need no acting experience, so we can round up a few people. And even if we can't, the play can go on. If it comes to it, Lily and I can stand in costume with the headbands to represent the soldiers."

"But Shimada will be suspicious."

"Of what?" Lily asks.

"I told you yesterday. I had to make up a story about Chen and his men filling in at short notice because the other extras quit. If they're not in the play, Shimada will wonder why."

"Is that all?"

"What do you mean?" Peterson's voice sounds confident, but his eyes shift nervously from Lily to Hill and back.

"My walk last night took me to the hospital for bandages. On the way back I took a detour to avoid a Japanese patrol. I ended up near the Japanese embassy—where you were having a conversation with Shimada." She stops talking and stares at him. "What was the conversation about, Neil?"

Peterson shuffles uncomfortably under her unrelenting stare. "I was arranging a visa for you," he finally admits.

"There's a gunboat leaving tomorrow that will take us downriver to where we can get a steamer to San Francisco. I wanted it to be a surprise. I was going to tell you after the play."

"The surprise would have been yours. I don't need a visa. I'm staying here."

"You can't."

"I can, and I will. America is your country. You go home. But China is my country. I'm staying here."

"But you'll be safe in America." A whine has entered Peterson's voice. He looks desolate. "You're only one person. What can you do here?"

"I don't know," she replies with a rueful smile, "but something. Even if it's just changing bandages or comforting a dying boy or talking to a woman who's just been raped—something."

"I love you, Lily." Peterson takes a step forward, but the expression on her face stops him cold.

"You don't love me. You love the idea of loving me—the idea of having a beautiful Chinese girl to show off at parties in America. To show people how open-minded you are and how much you care about the poor Chinese."

"That's not true."

"Isn't it? What were you and Shimada really talking about?"

"What do you mean? A visa—I told you."

"Shimada's not a man who will do anything for free. What did you offer him for the visa?"

"Nothing." Peterson's sweating freely now and clenching and unclenching his fists. "I didn't offer him anything."

"Answer my question." Shimada's pistol is in her hand and pointed at Peterson's head. There's shuffling behind them as the other actors flee the stage.

Peterson's eyes bulge in fear. "Don't shoot! Don't shoot! Please."

"I won't," Lily says, her voice icy, "if you tell me what I want to know."

"Okay, okay. I told Shimada about Chen and his soldiers." The barrel of the gun doesn't waver. "I *had* to. Shimada was suspicious anyway after the rehearsal. And Masao was coming to the play. He would have realized immediately that Chen and the others weren't refugees. I only derived a benefit from something that was going to happen anyway. I did it for you, Lily. For us."

"No, you did it for yourself."

Lily moves forward until the barrel of the pistol is touching Peterson's forehead.

"Lily, no," Hill says.

She ignores him. The three stand like statues on the empty stage for what seems like an age. Then Lily pulls the trigger.

The click of the hammer coming down on the empty chamber is followed immediately by Peterson's sobs as he collapses to his knees.

Lily lowers the pistol. "I took the bullets out of it last night," she says. "I didn't want an accident."

Peterson looks up, red-eyed and pale. "Thank you," he murmurs.

"Don't thank me," she replies. "You made a decision. You chose to betray Chen and the others. Whether things were going to happen anyway is irrelevant. You made the decision to sacrifice twelve men. You chose that they be massacred. That they weren't has nothing to do with you. You are going to have to live with your choice for the rest of your life. I wish you luck." She pockets the pistol and turns to Hill. "We should go. There's nothing left for us here."

Hill nods and the two of them walk off the stage, leaving Peterson with his burden and his loneliness.

CHAPTER EIGHTEEN

Ashford, Ohio

Present Day

Pike shoved the cooler as far into the WRX as he could and slammed the hatch. With the backseats folded down there was a lot of space, but Pike had filled it with everything he thought he might need on his road trip to the west coast. Theresa's two modest suitcases also didn't help, but he would regain that space when he dropped her off at the airport.

"We in good time?" Pike asked as he climbed into the driver's seat.

"We're good," she replied. "I printed out my boarding pass last night, so I'm all set." She looked over her shoulder for a last glimpse of the house as Pike pulled out onto the road. "I'm going to miss this place."

"Yeah," Pike agreed. "It's been a roller coaster. Mind you, my body's going to thank me for getting away from the lifestyle I led here."

"Wait until you get to California and the coke culture and cheap dope."

"Nah. This is a new me—clean-living and hardworking. Shit, I might even lose weight. I'm going to do what *I* want."

"How did your dad take the news that you were kicked out of school and heading for the beach?"

"Not well. We've talked three times. The first call was short—he hung up on me. The second was longer—mostly him telling me what an idiot I was for blowing my one chance at the perfect life. The third call was better. He let me explain my plans for studying Asian history. He didn't approve, but he wished me luck. He even offered to send some money, but I said no."

"Really! You said no to the money?"

Pike nodded as he turned the car onto the airport road. "If I sell the car and steer clear of shady Harrys and blue bars, I should have enough to last for a while. Then I'll pick up something to make ends meet. Never again do I want the pressure of someone else saying what I should or shouldn't do." He smiled at her. "What about you? How will you make ends meet?"

Theresa laughed. "I'm an actress. That's code for making ends meet. I've got some contacts in Beijing. That should get me some auditions, and I'll work up from there. In my spare time I'll try to find out what happened to my family."

"New beginnings for both of us."

Pike and Theresa sat in silence, remembering the first and only performance of *The Third Act* and its tragic aftermath.

Pike spoke first. "Do you think Tone was right with all that stuff he said about choices and decisions?"

She thought for a minute as the airport tower loomed into view. "To a degree. Obviously we all make choices and decisions every day, and we have to live with the consequences, even if those decisions lock us on to a certain path or hurt the people around us. If Tone's theory about Peterson is correct, then his betrayal was a major decision that shaped the rest of his life..."

"But?" Pike prompted.

"Tone wanted his own life and the world around him to be more rational—more organized—than it can ever be. He wanted decisions to be simple and clear-cut, with well-defined consequences. He hated the idea that the world, especially the world of human relationships, is a messy place where shit sometimes happens for no obvious reason. That's why he focused on Allen's decisions to explain why I drifted away from him and Seeger's to explain why he couldn't go to MIT."

Pike pulled up in front of the door to the airport departure wing.

"I wonder sometimes," Theresa went on, "how much of Tone's intellectual arrogance and desire for order were masks to hide behind. Under the masks maybe there was just a scared little boy who couldn't stand the pressure of pretending anymore. Maybe the real Tone was actually terrified of going to MIT to become the famous physicist that everyone—including him—expected him to be. Maybe, without completely understanding why, Tone made that final decision to escape."

"That's pretty heavy stuff," Pike said. "Do you really think that's how it played out in his mind?"

Theresa shrugged. "I don't know. I'm not a psychologist. I'm just thinking about people's motivations. It's what actors do."

"Well, don't think too much about me."

Theresa opened the door, but before she could get out, Pike said, "Wait a minute. There's something I need to show you." He reached into his pocket and pulled out a crumpled piece of paper. "I've been carrying this around for weeks. I was going to show it to you at the funeral, but I chickened out. Since then there just hasn't been an appropriate moment. Perhaps there *is* no appropriate moment, but if I'm going to show it to you, I have to do it now." He smoothed it out as much as possible and passed it over. "It's an email Tone wrote that day. He sent it on delay, so I didn't get it until two days later."

Theresa looked at Pike with such sadness that he thought she was going to refuse to read it. But finally she took the paper.

Pike, my dear and only friend. I hope things have worked out as I planned. I intend for there to be only one death. The first two empty chambers are for Quigley and Seeger. I intend only to frighten them.

I came to this country confident (some would say arrogant) that my destiny was to do great things in physics. I was totally blind to everything else—the people around me, the culture I was in and the culture I had left behind. My work was all that mattered—more so even than Theresa, and for that I am truly sorry. She deserved better than me.

The acting, which you persuaded me to do, opened my eyes to many things, but too late. Had I discovered this side of myself as a boy, perhaps things would have been different. But what's the point of wondering about that? I can never embrace the messy world that Theresa once told me was where she drew her inspiration. My path was fixed and now it is destroyed. I can see no decisions that will alter that or set me on a different path. All that's left is the ultimate decision.

I hope you and Theresa can forgive me, and I wish you both everything you want in your futures, whatever that may be.

Goodbye, my friend.

Tone

Theresa stared long and hard at the note, tears running down her cheeks. At last she looked up at Pike. "Can I keep this?" she asked shakily.

"Of course," he said. "Are you going to be okay?" He put a hand on her arm.

She produced a tissue, dabbed her eyes and blew her nose. "I'll be okay," she said with a weak smile. "I've got plenty of time on the plane to think about things." She squeezed Pike's hand, climbed out of the car and stood forlornly on the sidewalk.

Pike got out, opened the hatch and hauled out her suitcases. He went around the car and stood awkwardly beside her. "Do you want me to come in with you?"

She shook her head. "I'll be okay," she repeated.

Pike moved in and they embraced, both fighting back tears.

"I'll email you when I get settled in Beijing," Theresa said when they drew apart.

"And don't you forget to keep checking my Facebook page," Pike replied. "I plan to upload some awesome pics of my epic road trip."

"I'll be right there with you." She extended the handles on her cases and headed toward the doors. Halfway there she turned. "Make good decisions, Pike, or at least ones you can reverse."

"You too," he said. "Bye."

"Bye."

Pike watched as she went through the doors and disappeared.

"You can't park here." A security guard was approaching.

"No sweat, man," Pike said, heading back to the driver's door. "This is just a pit stop. I'm on my way." He closed the door, pulled away from the curb and headed out of the airport. Yeah, he said to himself, I'm on my way.

AUTHOR'S NOTE

The Third Act is a novel, but there is much truth in it. In the modern story it is a general truth. Many Asian students coming to study in colleges and universities in North America experience considerable stress. Much of this stems from the obvious cultural and linguistic differences, but a significant amount comes from a pressure to succeed, either brought by the students themselves or imposed by family and friends back home. How this stress is handled varies, and I have tried to show three possible outcomes in the ways this stress impacts Tone, Pike and Theresa.

The historical background to the Nanjing story and the massacre of late 1937 is accurate. It is based on accounts written by John Rabe and other Europeans who lived through the horrors and were instrumental in creating the Safety Zone that saved some 200,000 lives, and on a research visit to Nanjing where the walls breached by the invading Japanese, Jinling university and theatre, and Rabe's house still stand.

The novel is based on the original version of the script for the movie of the same name by Calvin Yao and it would not exist were it not for Calvin's idea. Thanks are also due to Gordon Mcghie of CG Bros Entertainment who got me involved in this remarkable project and to Eric Hu of Jaingsu Golden Oak Pictures who was my guide through Nanjing's streets and sad history. *The Third Act* is a much better work because of Janice Weaver's fine editing skills.

Born in Edinburgh, Scotland, JOHN WILSON grew up on the Isle of Skye and outside Glasgow without the slightest idea that he would ever write books. After completing a degree in geology at the University of St. Andrews, he worked in Zimbabwe and Alberta before taking up writing full time and moving out to Vancouver Island in 1991. John is the author of numerous articles, essays, poems, reviews and almost fifty novels and nonfiction books for kids, teens and adults. He was a finalist for the Governor General's Literary Award (*The Alchemist's Dream*, 2007), and his books have won or been short-listed for most Canadian children's literature prizes. For more information, visit johnwilsonauthor.com.